**Longarm drew his saddle gun
and rolled out of the saddle...**

Longarm turned to cover the gap in the cactus and, sure enough, heard approaching hoofbeats as whoever had been ghosting him spurred his own mount to keep from losing him entirely. So Longarm had the drop on Laredo, who tore through the same gap, not looking right or left, which was an awful mistake on his part. Longarm snapped, "All right, Laredo!"

Then he saw it wasn't Laredo, but some son of a bitch he'd never seen before. But since said son of a bitch was swinging the muzzle of a Remington his way as he reined in, Longarm fired first...

TABOR EVANS

LONGARM

ON THE SANTA CRUZ

A JOVE BOOK

LONGARM ON THE SANTA CRUZ

A Jove Book/published by arrangement with
the author

PRINTING HISTORY
Jove edition/June 1985

ISBN: 0-515-08254-6

PRINTED IN THE UNITED STATES OF AMERICA

LONGARM

ON THE SANTA CRUZ

Chapter 1

The pigeons roosting for the night in the belfry of St. Peter's were not alone as the sun went down behind the Front Range to the west, and the lamps of Denver began to light up all around down below. As a pigeon pooped on the brim of his battered Stetson, the dirty old man who had gone to roost with the not-too-tidy birds was a mite annoyed, but he didn't see fit to cuss. For he was still alive and free, which was a lot more than the two young fools who had ridden out of that botched bank job with him could say right now. He had warned them before the stickup not to head for the Denver Tenderloin if things went wrong, but some kids just refused to listen to their elders. So old Tulsa had been caught with his pants literally down in the establishment of madam Ruth Jacobs, and poor Billy Mansfield had been gunned by the law before he'd even made it to the back door of Emma Gould's house of ill repute.

The dirty old man in the belfry had managed to get old as well as dirty by acting seven times more cautious than the cold-blooded crustacean he was nicknamed after, although he seldom answered to Crawdad McGraw in public, of late. The name was on too many Wanted posters. But there was still a lot to be said for scooting for cover like a crawdad, backing into a hole the law wasn't likely to suspicion, and staying there no matter what, until it was safe for a fact to put even a feeler out.

Another pigeon pooped on him with a contented coo and this time he indulged his carefully controlled emotions by muttering, "Just you wait, bird. I had time to grab a canteen on the fly. But I didn't bring no grub and as soon as I get hungry enough for raw poultry, I'll likely shit *you* afore it's safe to leave this stinksome hole in the sky!"

A shaft of light lanced through the belfry grillwork at a new and thus suspicious angle. So McGraw moved over to the grill for a look-see, gun in hand. He relaxed when he saw it was just a gal in a dormer window across the street. She was dressed townee and fashionably, the way gals in this more fancy part of Denver were supposed to. She had likely just come home from work or whatever. She had moved the lamp over to her dressing table and was taking off her hat. Her figure sure looked handsome with her hands up like that. He wondered if her hat was all she aimed to take off. It was too early for anyone to be fixing to get in bed, alone, but some gals changed their duds if they meant to go out again after work, and . . . Lord have mercy, she was unbuttoning her bodice, sure as hell!

The dirty parts of the dirty old man responded wistfully as the she-male form across the way peeled off her calico summer frock and sat down at the dressing table, bare back to him, while long black hair came unpinned for a slow and somehow sensuous brushing. The owlhoot peeping from the dark belfry licked his lips and murmured, "Hot damn, you ain't going out again after all, are you, honey? You're in for the night and there's no call at all for you to draw your blinds, with your bedroom window facing nothing but this

2

pure old church tower! I sure hope it's sort of hot and stuffy over there, under that slate roofing. For I know if *I* was a pretty young gal sleeping alone in high summer, I wouldn't want to mess with no hot and scratchy nightgown!"

The crawdad part of the sly old outlaw's nature warned him to simmer down. But, what the hell, what harm could it do even a crawdad to watch a pretty gal undress, from safe in his hidey-hole?

He didn't dare smoke. He was already a mite hungry. And he hadn't had a woman for a wistfully long time. He'd been too slick to be taken like Tulsa and Billy. He'd known the minute he'd detected that shifty look in the eyes of the old gal he'd meant to hide out with, up here in the better part of town, that she meant to turn him in for the considerable price on his gray head. So when she'd gone down to the corner grocery, she said, he'd lit out the back way and let himself in this nearby church he'd noticed on an earlier visit. Only young and stupid gents in his line of work *trusted* womankind. But, Lord have mercy, the critters were so comforting to have nearby in other ways, and that old gal he'd thought he might be able to trust had lit out to call the law on him before he'd even gotten to steal a feel.

He decided the gal across the way was much prettier and more to his liking, even though, in truth, he couldn't make out her features from this range. He could see that she had a better figure and, as he looked down at the deserted street between them, he didn't see how she could call the law on anybody, unless he was dumb enough to fall asleep.

The crawdad in his old gray head snorted in disgust and said, "Sure, you just go over and help yourself to some of that whilst she screams loud enough to wake the dead and, even if she don't, then what? You think a dusty old coot like you could go in or out without the neighbors talking?"

His dirty parts listened to his smart parts, but it wasn't easy. For now the young gal across the way had finished

3

combing her hair and she was standing up and hauling off her chemise and turning about to face his way, bare-titted, as she walked right toward him in only her underdrawers and stockings.

The girl moved to the window as if to draw the blinds. Crawdad McGraw pleaded aloud, "Please don't let her, God! There's no reason to go to bed stuffsome on such a warm night unless there's other windows facing yourn!"

The girl framed in the window seemed to be staring thoughtfully right at him. But since all she could see was the innocent façade of the church tower, she turned back with a little shrug and moved to her brass bedstead, sitting on the counterpane to roll down her stockings, slowly, almost as if she knew some poor bastard was watching her with a raging erection and she sort of enjoyed the notion.

By the time she'd finished, and rose again to slip off her loose silk underdrawers, the dirty old man watching her had his greasy fly unbuttoned and was masturbating madly with his gun back in its holster as he braced himself with one hand against the grillwork. She was now stark naked as she moved over to pick up the lamp. As she turned, with the lamp illuminating the dark V between her shapely thighs, McGraw pleaded, "Don't put out that lamp, honey! Not yet! For God's sake, let me see all you has to offer!"

She didn't trim her lamp. She placed it on the bed table and lay down facing the dirty old man. She spread her bare thighs for full inspection and began to stroke herself slowly between them as if she, too, had needs there was no other way for a lonely and sensuous person to satisfy.

And so, as two total strangers masturbated in unison with the space of a churchyard and street between them, the crawdad part of McGraw's brain paid no attention to the uneasy fluttering of wings about him in the dark.

Something cold and metallic pressed firmly against the

4

sweaty nape of Crawdad McGraw's neck and a deep but pleasant enough voice announced, "You are under arrest for the attempted robbery of the Drover's Trust and other crimes too numerous to mention."

The old owlhoot stiffened and seriously considered the gun at his side even as he felt it being lifted from its holster.

"Don't be silly. You can put your pecker back in your pants and turn around now, McGraw," the voice said.

The murderous old man sighed and did so. As he saw who'd just gotten the drop on him, illuminated oddly by the patchwork of lamplight from across the way, he sighed. "I might have knowed it was *you*, Longarm. But *how?* I'm sure nobody saw me break in downstairs, and there was nobody in the church when I made for the ladder up from the choir loft."

Deputy U. S. Marshal Custis Long said, "Hold out your hands. For I mean to cuff a slippery old cuss like you."

As the owlhoot reluctantly allowed the taller and younger man to cuff his wrists, Longarm stared over McGraw's shoulder at the gal putting on the bawdy show across the way. "I must say my new deputy puts her heart into her work," he said. "Look at the way that pretty little thing strums her old banjo! I can't tell from here if she thinks I'm still creeping up the ladder at you or if she's just naturally horny-natured. But I sure see why it was so easy to get the drop on you just now!"

McGraw gasped and said, "You son of a bitch! I might have knowed it was a ruse! But how in the hell did you get an innocent gal just living across the street by accident to trick me so disgusting?"

"I never divulge trade secrets to the other side, Crawdad. Catching you was enough trouble as it was. Move over to the trap and ease down the ladder while I cover you. Don't get any sudden silly notions near the bottom. I got Dutch and Smiley waiting in the choir loft and, if you know *my* rep, you'll know better than to give *them* rascals an excuse to gun you!"

"How can I go down the ladder with my infernal hands cuffed, damn it?"

"Carefully, old timer. You won't fall unless you let go of the rungs. If you do, you won't get far, so don't."

Crawdad McGraw took Longarm's advice to heart and a few minutes later they were down below, where Longarm holstered his own .44-40 and handed the prisoner's older Colt '74 to Deputy Smiley. Smiley was the morose breed's name. Nobody had ever seen him smile. But his shorter and stockier partner, Dutch, was grinning as he told McGraw, "They got a new patent gallows the hangman's been just dying to try out, old son."

The prisoner told him to do a dreadfully disrespectful thing to his mother. But before Dutch could pistol-whip McGraw, Longarm said, "Don't rawhide the poor cuss, Dutch. He's got enough on his plate. I want you boys to deliver him alive and well to the federal house of detention across town. I got to go make sure the lady I asked to help us out is all right. I promised her a full explanation once we made the arrest."

Smiley said nothing as he took McGraw by one arm, but Dutch asked, "No fooling, did she really put on a peep show for this old rascal, Longarm?"

Longarm shrugged. "Well, she did seem to be holding his undivided attention, like I asked her to before we circled the block to pussy-foot in through the same back door this rascal found as easy to pick. I disremember giving her exact instructions, but she seems a natural-born actress."

"She was jerking off naked in bed!" cackled Crawfish McGraw as they all headed for the stairs.

Longarm grimaced in distaste. "Pay him no mind, boys,"

he said. "Get him over to the lock-up before he corrupts your morals entire, and . . . Dutch?"

"Yeah?"

"I meant what I said about him getting there in shape to stand trial. I know that guard at the Drover's Trust was a drinking pard of yours, but we ain't paid by the taxpayers of these United States to let our feelings show!"

Dutch said grudgingly that he wouldn't gun the son of a bitch unless he refused to come along quietly. So they all parted friendly in the churchyard and Longarm went across the street to knock on the downstairs door of the building Crawdad McGraw had recently been so interested in.

It took some time for Mrs. Petunia Snow to make it down from the usually empty maid's room in her garret and, of course, she'd put some duds on in the meanwhile, or at least she was wearing a terry-cloth robe when she let Longarm in, giggling.

She asked, "Was he really across the way in that belfry as you suspected, Deputy Long?"

Longarm nodded soberly. "You can call me Custis, seeing as we know one another better now, Miss Petunia. I didn't suspicion old McGraw was hiding up in Saint Pete's. I was close to certain of it. Like I told you before, the police informant he went to first lives only a block and a half away, and there just ain't many places in the respectable parts of town a dirty old stranger could hide out. Saint Pete's is R.C. and we knew he was a lapsed Roman Catholic. He began his life of crime as a choirboy, robbing poor boxes. Then he had to leave another town, sudden, after attacking a nun."

"He does sound disgusting. But since I heard no shots just now, you must have taken him alive, right?"

"We did, thanks to you, Miss Petunia. I figured as soon as I saw how close the church was to his last known address that an ex-choirboy would know when and how to sneak

7

into such an establishment. I figured he'd make for the belfry as the only place he wasn't likely to meet up with others during services. I didn't have to figure, I *knew,* that going head first up a ladder after an armed and dangerous killer could be mighty injurious to one's health. So, as you recall, my first move was to go to your back door and ask your permission to look out your upstairs window, for openers."

The shapely brunette widow woman giggled some more and led him into her study off the hall as she said, "I recall indeed. I must say I was rather shocked when you asked if I'd be willing to distract his attention for you just after sundown. But when you told me about all the innocent people the nasty old thing had killed I . . . well, just had to do my duty. Did I do it *right,* Custis?"

She sank gracefully down onto a sofa and patted it for him to do likewise. So he tossed his hat aside and did so, saying soberly, "You did indeed, Miss Petunia. I'd tell you what *he* was doing when I just walked up behind him, gun in hand, but I wouldn't want to shock your delicate ears."

She said, "Call me Petty. It's what my late husband always called me. I don't know why on earth my mother named me *Petunia!* And as for my delicate ears, you said once you'd made your arrest you'd tell me everything. So what *was* he doing while he was playing peeping tom with me, Custis?"

Longarm looked down, a tactical error, since she hadn't fastened the front of her robe too well. "He was doing what most peeping toms might be expected to be doing at such times," he told her.

She laughed, sort of lewdly, and said, "Good. It serves him right. I was *trying* to tease the nasty brute."

"You surely did, Petty. You did yourself proud as my temporary deputy, and like I said, there'll be some reward money in it for you, once we get the paperwork in order."

She looked suddenly concerned and asked, "Oh, dear,

8

will you have to put down that I was in a state of undress on duty?"

He chuckled and said, "Not hardly. I'll word it so's my report just shows you cooperated in the investigation by letting us use your top-story window. That's the simple truth, when you study on it."

It was her turn to laugh as she said, "I must confess I may have gotten a bit carried away with my act. Could you see *everything* I was doing to tease him, from across the way?"

"To tell the truth," he lied, "it was sort of hard to make out just what might or might not be going on across the way, with the lamplight so dim and the maid's window so small." Then, in hopes of changing the awkward subject, he added, "Whatever happened to your maid and the other serving help as usually goes with a house this size?"

She sighed and said, "I let all my help go after my husband died almost a year ago. It was partly financial prudence, but mostly to give my hands something to do. You've no idea how much time a recent widow woman has on her hands, Custis. You and your deputies were the first gentlemen callers I've had in recent memory."

Then she took his big brown hand in hers and placed it firmly in her lap as she added, "Speaking of hands, what you might have thought you saw me doing with my own upstairs was only funning. I wouldn't want you to leave here with the notion I indulged in self-abuse!"

As she began to rock *his* hand back and forth in the terry-cloth cradle of her lap, he couldn't help noticing that her robe was sort of falling open down there, and it was abusing the hell out of *him*. "I can see why you like to be called Petty, though I know you'd never pet yourself so hard," he said. "But, no offense, Miss Petty, you're making it hard as hell for me to recall I'm supposed to be a proper gentleman, on duty, leastwise."

9

She giggled, leaned back, and spread her thighs as she hauled his hand all the way inside her robe with one of her hands while she groped for him with the other. As his questing fingers found her lust-slicked slit she found her way to his fly and murmured, "Oh, I do seem to be making it hard for you, and they do say doing things like this by *hand* is a wicked vice that can drive one crazy, so . . ."

So he kissed her, hard, as she hauled his hard-on out, and they went crazy as hell together for a while. When they came together the second time, having somehow meanwhile wound up on the rug with their heads in the most fortunately unlit fireplace across the room, Petty sighed. "Don't you think this would work better in bed, without that scratchy tweed vest of yours against my poor bare tum-tum, dear?" Petty asked.

He laughed, kissed her some more, and replied, "Well, I never told them other deputies anything about seeing them no more this side of office hours, and I can see you need me more than my office possibly could at this hour."

So he helped her to her feet and she led him to her bedroom lest he suddenly change his mind and make a break for it. He had no such uncivil intent toward the lady. For now that they'd sort of broken the ice, getting undressed together was sort of like two old loving pards getting down to serious business. As he entered her again on the bed, with her hips braced on a pillow and his old organ grinder knowing the way home better, she laughed and said, "Oh, that feels so lovely, Custis! I'd almost forgotten how good the real thing feels, my year of mourning still having a good six weeks to go!"

He felt sort of wistful about the gentlemen callers she'd no doubt be entertaining indeed in the near future. But meanwhile he suspected she had to be telling the truth about not having had a man for some time. For the considerable effort he'd already put into her on that rug hadn't slowed

10

her down at all in bed and, in truth, starting over from scratch in this more comfortable position seemed to be inspiring him to new heights as well.

She came ahead of him this time, however. "Stop. I want to try something new," she panted.

She got on top, bounced on him a few times the right way to assure his undivided interest, then said shyly, "I must confess I have been naughty, spending so many nights alone of late. It must be true that self-abuse drives people a little crazy. For in my quest for self-satisfaction, I've been having the most wicked thoughts."

He smiled up at her understandingly and said, "I know. Ain't it amazing what folks can dream up as they're stroking themselves to sleep?"

She blushed becomingly from her bare nipples up as she went on bouncing, slow and teasing. "Surely a man who's not in mourning has no call for crimes against nature, Custis!" she exclaimed.

He blushed a mite himself as he replied, "I ain't sure it's a crime, no matter what the preachers say, and I don't believe they really mean it themselves. For it's an established fact of nature that nine out of ten folks play with themselves on occasion and the tenth one is a liar."

She giggled like a mean little kid and reached down between them to stroke her untouched parts, her nails in his pubic hair. She avoided his eyes with her own as she confided, "I love to rock the Indian in the canoe, even when I've got the real thing in me, deep. But please close your eyes, dear. It's embarrassing to do that with someone watching!"

He laughed. "That well may be, but as long as we're confessing our secret vices, you know damn well, and how, that I know you get a thrill out of it."

She giggled again. "I see a girl can keep no secrets from you. But I feel so wicked letting you watch, and ... Oh,

11

yesssss! I am going crazy, but I just don't care!"

It was driving him sort of crazy, too, since despite the inspiring all-out passion of her performance, she wasn't moving enough on his shaft. So he rolled her over to do it right.

She moaned and began to masturbate harder as she hissed, "Yessss! Oh, my God, it feels so big, and I'm fixing to come again!"

That made two of them.

She jerked herself off with his shaft sliding in and out of her. They came together in a long, shuddering series of mutual pulsations.

As he rolled off her, Petty said, "Good heavens, you must think I'm a shameless slut, now, right?"

He put out a hand to stroke her naked flesh reassuringly as he replied, "Don't talk dumb. Where in the U.S. Constitution do it say a man who likes to screw is a hero, while a naturally warm-natured woman is something less?"

She laughed. "We have been acting sort of heroic, haven't we? I'm still trying to figure out how. I mean, I know what we've been doing, and I know we really ought to be ashamed of ourselves. But I still don't see how I could have simply thrown myself at you this evening! I know you won't believe this, but I haven't had any sex at all, with anyone, for almost a year!"

"You just answered your own question, honey," he said. "It only takes most folk a few nights, sleeping alone, to get horny as hell."

She dimpled down at his semi-sated shaft and said, "I know. I'd be ashamed to tell even you half the crazy things that go through a young widow woman's head when her late husband's fool friends feel it's too early to console her right. I fear I've acted disgraceful with even the ugly men I know—only in my head, of course. But I never dreamed,

12

when you politely knocked on my back door less than two or three hours ago, that you'd wind up actually in me and then some! God help the really wicked girls you must meet in your line of work!"

He laughed. "I'm too romantic-natured to enjoy the favors of your average tenderloin tart, Petty. I prefer the company of more innocent gals such as yourself."

"Oh, come on! You told me before that you'd arrested that old outlaw's companions earlier in houses of ill repute."

"I arrested one, in Ruth Jacobs's place. The one shot in the vicinity of Emma Gould's was taken by a less gentle cuss. I assure you, neither of us lawmen were visiting such unseemly neighborhoods with impure thoughts in our heads."

She began to stroke his semi-erection thoughtfully as she said, "I've heard of Ruth Jacobs. They say she's a terrible woman. Is it true she charges special rates for . . . ah . . . crimes against nature?"

"Most such establishments aim to please, Petty. If you're asking if I've ever had personal experience of the French lessons Ruth Jacobs is said to specialize in, I ain't. It would be unprofessional for a lawman to enjoy the professional favors of a police informant."

"Oh." She sighed, looking sort of disappointed. "Then you wouldn't be able to tell me if those bad girls go all the way, with their naughty kissing?"

That was too dumb a question to answer, so he didn't try. "I've always wondered, sort of, what it would be like to do such a dirty thing," she said. "You do agree it's dirty, don't you, dear?"

He said, "Cheating at cards against honest players is dirty. Lots of things is dirty. But I've never thought anything a man and a woman might want to do to one another, willing, could be all that dirty."

She sighed, closed her eyes, took a deep breath as if to

13

steel herself, and dove headfirst on his semi-erection, which didn't stay semi-erect long once she started bobbing her head and sucking like a greedy calf.

He knew at once she was lying, trying to pretend she'd never done anything like this before. But he didn't object to her delicate feelings, since it felt so good. She crawled higher on the bed to cock a leg across him, her parted thighs above his face, trembling with expectation. So the rest of the night got wild as hell and it was small wonder he overslept the sunrise.

Chapter 2

Longarm got to the federal building downtown about a quarter after nine, walking sort of stiffly. The prissy clerk who played the typewriter in the front office glanced up at the clock as Longarm limped in. Longarm said, "I know, Henry. But if you'd been through what I been through, recent, you still wouldn't be here. I'd ask if the boss was in the back, but I'm sort of tired of dumb questions this morning."

He started for the oak door of his superior, U. S. Marshal William Vail. But the clerk hissed him over and half whispered, "Watch yourself, Longarm. I think you're really in trouble this morning!"

"What for? The office has only been open for business a few hours and I pulled overtime last night."

"We were looking all over town for you, too! Where the devil did you run off to after you arrested Crawdad McGraw?"

"I was questioning a possible federal witness, Henry. Didn't Dutch and Smiley deliver the prisoner to the lockup like I ordered 'em to?"

"They did not. Dutch shot him on the corner of Colfax and Broadway, in front of witnesses! Dutch says McGraw was trying to escape. The witnesses tell it different!"

Longarm shook his head wearily. "Oh, shit. I might have knowed." Then he went on back to face the music in the old man's private office.

Marshal Vail always growled at Longarm when he reported for duty, usually late. So Longarm knew the situation was serious when the pudgy older lawman smiled up at him almost pleasantly from behind the cluttered desk and said, "Sit down and tell me all about, old son."

Longarm took his usual seat in the leather guest chair across the desk from his boss and reached for a cheroot. "Ain't much to tell, Billy," he said. "I wasn't there. I put the cuffs on Crawdad McGraw around eight or a little later. Then I ordered Smiley and Dutch to deliver him to the house of detention for me. I never even heard the shots."

Vail leaned back in his swivel chair. "There was only one. Dutch must have held the muzzle right to the back of McGraw's shirt, judging from the powder burns. Smiley had the sense to take off the prisoner's cuffs, after. But unfortunately a mess of people saw him doing so. Don't never shoot a prisoner trying to escape at a main intersection, early in the evening, on a warm one for strolling, if you don't want a mess of witnesses."

"I'll try to remember that, Billy. I'd best have a few words with the indiscreet rascals. Where are Dutch and Smiley now?"

"Suspended, pending the findings of the coroner's jury, of course. The damned fools gunned a man cold-blooded on the streets of Denver, making it Denver's jurisdiction, damn it to hell! How many times do I have to tell you boys that even a federal officer is subject to local law if he breaks it, or that homicide's a matter local law takes considerable interest in?"

16

Longarm lit his smoke, shook out the match, and said, "Don't get your bowels in an uproar at *me*, Billy. I left McGraw alive and well last night. I never saw what happened on the way down the slope from Capitol Hill. So the local law has nothing on me one way or the other, right?"

"Wrong. The coroner means to call you in as a witness."

"A witness to what? I didn't see or even hear a goddamned thing! I *told* Dutch not to hurt the old bastard!"

Vail nodded grimly. "With good reason. Smiley told me why. He don't talk much but, as you know, when Smiley does talk, he always tells the truth, even when he ain't under oath. If the coroner's jury gets it out of Smiley that you mentioned Dutch being pals with a man McGraw gunned, there's no way on earth to make it sound impulsive instead of premeditated. So tell me how many other gents in town might or might not know Dutch had been close with one of McGraw's recent victims."

Longarm blew a thoughtful smoke ring. "Ain't sure anybody knew it but me," he told his boss. "I only knew because the three of us was drinking in the Parthenon together one day recent."

Vail nodded. "Good. If the matter don't come up, Smiley will know better than to volunteer the information, and a trigger-happy deputy with no particular motive has a certain leeway with a coroner's jury. It was an established fact McGraw was dangerous and, hell, he might have *looked* like he was about to make a break for it, to a poor dumb innocent boy with a hair-trigger S&W in his inexperienced hand."

Longarm blinked and asked, "You call Dutch *inexperienced?*"

Vail said, "I do when and if I'm called afore a coroner's jury. I don't want 'em asking you how come you turned a homicidal maniac over to a green deputy or just what orders regarding the same you may or may not have given the poor

17

callow youth. So I'm sending you out of town on a mission more serious than a mere *pro forma* discussion of dead skunks."

He rummaged among the papers on his cluttered desk and found a sheaf of papers to hand across to Longarm. As the younger deputy leaned back to scan the first page, Vail said, "You can read all that on the train. It's a pain in the ass to sit still whilst a slow reader reads dozens of pages. How come you read so slow, Longarm?"

"I don't, when it's the *Police Gazette*. But I don't like to miss any of the fine print in a crime report."

"You'll have plenty of time after you leave, then. For I'm sending you this time to the Arizona Territory. A band of owlhoots in the same line of work as the late Crawdad McGraw has been raising ned with the banks along the Rio Santa Cruz, so—"

"Jesus Christ!" Longarm cut in. "You're sending me down to the Arizona desert in high summer? It's hot enough up here on the High Plains! Why can't I take my paid vacation somewhere sensible, like Pike's Peak or, hell, the Alaska Territory, if you want me *really* out of town?"

Billy Vail smiled grimly and replied, "It ain't that easy. I can't send one of my men into another federal marshal's jurisdiction without written approval. Fortunately, the U. S. Marshal riding herd on that God-forsook part of the world rode with me in the Rangers when the world was younger and greener. So he says you're welcome to poke about down there all you want. Him and his own deputies have already given up on a somewhat cold trail."

"You call the cactus country along the Santa Cruz *cold*, Billy?"

"Well, whatever it is, nobody's been able to cut the owlhoots' trail after their last bank job a couple of weeks ago. But, hell, you scouted for the army before you started working for me, and now that I've brung you up smart..."

"Flattery don't count when it's over the line into pure bullshit!" Longarm declared, waving the top crime report. "This says they held up the Maricopa bank just before closing time. One got shot before he could mount up, but the rest rode clear somewheres. This says the resulting posse never cut trail one as they circled the whole township, no doubt sweating like hogs. This says the stickup took place seventeen days ago, not no two weeks, and you expect me to read sign *now,* after a whole mess of lawmen couldn't, way back when?"

Vail nodded and said, "Had they been any good at reading sign they'd have cut the trail, damn it. Everybody saw the rascals ride out of town in a cloud of dust, and it stands to reason they had to be *going* someplace. It ain't like the Arizona desert is a wooded area or a swamp, you know. It's mighty hard to hide a mounted band behind a cactus or a stirrup-high clump of greasewood. The water holes average forty miles apart, and unless they was mounted on hobby horses their mounts required graze as well as water. But them dumb Maricopa possemen just rode about in circles, looking for hoofprints in the sands of time, when they should have been studying on the nearest grass and water not occupied by settlers or Injuns."

"I've seen how a posse of townees can chase its own tail to nowheres, Billy. But by now any sign they missed is still long gone. That gang's had time to graze their mounts *fat* and send all the money home to mamma by now!"

Vail handed over a small, crisp bit of paper. "You can't keep this. But you'll find its serial number along with others in those other notes. As you can see, it's a U. S. Government Bond, issued at four percent interest and half matured. It was cashed this week in Tucson at two percent less than face value. Before that it resided in the vault of the bank held up further down the Santa Cruz, in Maricopa."

Longarm started to say something dumb. Then he nodded. "Yep, it does say 'Payable to the Bearer on Demand,' and any banker who forecloses on widows and orphans just for practice would see the modest profit to be made by cashing this and holding her to full maturity. Naturally, nobody at the bank in Tucson can rightly say just who they cashed this one for?"

"Naturally. The Treasury Department broadcast lists of the stolen bonds right after they was stolen. But, like you said, a two-percent profit is a two-percent profit, and the gang rode off with over fifty thousand dollars' worth of that government paper!"

Longarm handed the bond back, saying, "All right, so far they've only cashed one, for twenty-five. Why can't Treasury simply stop payment on all the ones as ain't been cashed yet, seeing they have the numbers on record and the bonds can't be in the hands of honest men at the moment?"

"I asked Treasury that, too," Vail said. "They said it's hard enough to sell paper, even at four percent, unless it's good as gold. They *have* to back 'em, just as they'd have to back stolen paper dollars, lest the credit rating of Uncle Sam go wobble-kneed. There's another reason. If Treasury just devalued stolen paper, who'd ever *hang on* to it long enough to get caught?"

Longarm took a thoughtful drag on his cheroot and nodded. "Makes sense. At least we don't have to worry about the bank robbers tossing the rest of them bonds to the desert winds. But so far, they only seem to have tried to cash one, for a small amount."

Vail said, "That's easy. The Maricopa bank job netted the gang twenty thousand in cash and fifty thousand in them harder to spend bonds. When they divvied up after their getaway their leader likely told 'em not to cash any of the government bonds for a spell. But there's always an asshole riding with any gang."

"I never asked how come somebody cashed one so early,"

Longarm said. "My comment was occasioned by the fact someone cashed it in Tucson and Tucson is on the Rio Santa Cruz, too. About eighty miles from Maricopa, without looking at the map. So they didn't have to worry about water or even grazing if they've simply been riding up and down a *river,* right?"

"It won't work that simple," Vail said. "I told you the local law down there has about given up. But before they did they naturally went through the standard motions. The Santa Cruz ain't just a desert river. It's thickly settled. But save for that bond turning up in Tucson, not a soul along the Santa Cruz seems to have noticed any mounted gangs riding by of late."

Longarm shrugged. "Hell, how far out in the desert would you have to circle to avoid a home spread or village? If they split up between jobs, they don't have to ride by *anyone* in a *gang.* There's two sides to every river, and who keeps detailed records of a drifting saddle tramp riding past on their own side of the same?" He took another drag on his smoke and added, "Then, too, if some only apparently innocent settler was renting rooms or watering horses sort of expensive, and not reporting it or even remembering it to the local law . . ."

Vail folded his pudgy hands across his expensive vest and leaned back even further as he fondly observed, "I do so enjoy watching a usually lazy deputy turning into a redbone hound sniffing for game scent, old son. But before I slips your leash, I hope you savvy I don't want you back before that coroner's jury adjourns for keeps? Take plenty of time and make sure you catch ever' one of the rascals."

Longarm snorted in disgust and said, "I'll be lucky if I catch *one* before I'm due for retirement. But I may as well get cracking."

"Good. I'll have Henry type up your travel orders before noon and you can catch the one o'clock southbound. You'll

21

naturally want to start from Maricopa, pick up a mount at the Gila Agency, and work your way up the Santa Cruz, right?"

Longarm frowned and asked, "Whatever for? The last sign they left was in Tucson, and the Southern Pacific will get me there first. I'll borrow a pony at the San Xavier Reserve and just start my investigation from well up the Santa Cruz."

Vail sighed and said, "I wish it was easier to bullshit you, Longarm. I don't *want* you back in less'n two weeks, damn it!"

A good part of Billy Vail's problem was solved just getting Longarm from Denver to Tucson. The rail connections were tedious as hell. Longarm had to take the Denver & Rio Grande all the way south to El Paso for openers, and when the friendly redhead traveling alone got off at Albuquerque he just had to let her go as pure as he'd met her. For though they *said* the Santa Fe would someday run its tracks west of Demming, someday hadn't come yet and you still had to take the long way 'round.

At El Paso he had time for a shave and a haircut before he boarded the Southern Pacific west for Tucson. There wasn't even an *ugly* woman to talk to in the coach, and the long hot dusty ride was boring as hell. When the train stopped at Douglas to change engines he was tempted to get off. Douglas was a boarder town, and bank robbers had been known to head for Mexico. But he wasn't paid to be impulsive and while Douglas lay on the Mexican line there was nothing much south of it but hot dry desert and hot-tempered Yaqui, while the Rio Santa Cruz, further west, offered a better watered route south and, if a rider was really desperate, a crack at the headwaters of the Mexican Rio de la Concepcion. Longarm had standing orders to stay out of Mexico since last he'd almost started another war with El

Presidente Diaz. But it was something to think about. So he stayed aboard the infernal train.

A million years later, or at least late at night according to his pocketwatch, he got off at last in Tucson. It wasn't quite as late once he'd set his watch back from Denver time to local time, but he still felt as tired as if he'd walked the whole way. Sitting still on a dusty coach seat wore a man's ass out worse than any saddle could. But before he could check into a hotel and soak his bones back into shape, he had to pay the usual courtesy call on the local law. So he headed up the dimly lit main street in the not-so-cool of evening. By the time he got to the town marshal's office, his long legs were starting to work right again.

Vail had wired ahead that he was coming, damn him, so the Tucson deputy marshal on night duty wasn't surprised to see him. "You'll want a look at the body, right?" he asked.

Longarm frowned and asked, "What body are we talking about, pard? Nobody mentioned a recent killing in your fair city to me before I left Denver."

The town law got up from behind his desk. "Oh, that's right. You must have been aboard the train when we found the rascal this afternoon. He was deposited in the city dump by a person or persons unknown, without a dumping permit, cuss their untidy souls. Come on, I'll show you. He's on ice at the undertaker *cum* county coroner's, just down the street."

As they went back outside the town law asked where Longarm's baggage might be. The taller deputy explained that he'd left his army saddle, Winchester, and possibles checked at the depot for now. The town marshal said, "I wouldn't leave 'em there overnight if I was you. We do the best we can, but Tucson is a caution when it comes to thieving. The Mexicans is bad enough, but the local Injuns make your average Mex *ladrones* look like pillars of the

23

community! They ain't supposed to walk the streets of town after dark, let alone get drunk in our many saloons. But how the hell can you say for sure a Papago or even a neatly dressed Apache ain't a ragged-ass Mexican?"

"Ain't we a mite west of Apache country, pard?"

"Tell that to an Apache with itchy feet. They ain't supposed to be here in Papago country. The Papago hates Apache worse than I do, and I can't *stand* the sons of bitches. But to get back to your baggage, it won't matter much to you whether it's stole by Papago, Apache, Mex, or just a naturally sticky-fingered white boy, for we hardly ever *catch* the sons of bitches."

"Where do they fence all the gear they seem so interested in?" Longarm asked.

"Hell, anywhere they can, of course. We naturally keep our eyes on the pawnshops. But many a gent in the market for a new saddle or, better yet, a gun, will be glad to hand out drinking money for the same in any handy alley."

"But you don't know for sure of any full-time receiver of stolen goods hereabouts? I've got a reason for asking."

"I know you have. We've been wondering why that stole government bond was cashed at a bank, where it would be reported as stole sooner than many a hock shop might have. It ain't hard to figure. What shylock's about to cash a bond he only stands to make a two-percent profit on after he holds it, hot, until it matures?"

Longarm took out two cheroots, handed one to the know-it-all, and lit them both up before he said, "Fences don't pay face value. They won't even take hot *money* unless the thief's willing to settle for a fraction he can safely spend. Paper as hot as we're discussing could be bought just the way one buys a stolen saddle *without* a serial number to fret about, for mere drinking money."

The town law frowned thoughtfully. "By gum, you're right. You're *good*, too! Not even my boss thought of that,

24

and he's supposed to know what he's doing."

Longarm shrugged and didn't answer. One of the things that made law enforcement so interesting west of the Big Muddy was the casual way most local governments hung badges on almost anyone who would work cheap.

They got to the funeral parlor and went in. Longarm noted how late it stayed open for business and, as they passed through a showroom full of empty caskets, wondered why. In most towns this size the local undertaker had to double selling hardware and such to make ends meet. Apparently Tucson lived up to its reputation as an easy town to die in.

The soberly dressed gent who had heard the front door open and came out from the rear to greet them looked prosperous as well as sort of spooky. Longarm wasn't spooked by undertakers, as a rule. He'd once made love to one of the she-male persuasion. But this one looked like one of his own customers and, when the town law introduced them, he *shook* like a cooled-off corpse as well.

But he seemed friendly enough as he led them back to his workshop, if that was what you called it. A naked Mexican lady who might have been a lot prettier in life lay atop a zinc-topped table with a ghastly hole in her skull. The undertaker noted Longarm's curiosity and explained, "Domestic tragedy. Her own family's paying for her funeral, since her husband hasn't been seen in town since he hit her with that ax. As soon as the embalming fluid firms her flesh some I mean to pretty her up with mortician's wax. I keep it in every flesh color. It's surprising how much a dirt-poor peon's willing to pay for a proper wedding or funeral."

Longarm suppressed a grimace and said, "I was given to understand you had a *male* cadaver here for me to look at, Doc."

The undertaker nodded, moved to what looked like a bank of filing cases set against one wall, and hauled out

25

what turned out to be a long metal drawer, half filled with cracked ice, rock salt, and a fully dressed corpse. Longarm moved closer. The body was that of a white youth of nineteen or twenty, dressed cow, but sort of nondescript. The dead boy's eyes were open and there was a puzzled little smile on his lips, as if he felt a mite surprised to find himself in such an odd position, but not really all that upset about it. The undertaker muttered, "Shit, rigor mortis is starting to set in. Come morning, he'll be grinning like a fiend from hell. But it's not as if anyone figures to claim him before we plant him in potter's field, and I had my assistants take a photograph of him for the files while his face was still fresh-killed. We're up-to-date in Tucson. Want to see his death certificate, Deputy Long?"

"I'll take your word on the autopsy report, Doc."

The undertaker looked confused. "Autopsy? On a corpse with its back full of bulletholes? Who gunned him might be a mystery, Deputy Long, but there was no mystery at all about the cause of death. He was shot in the spine once, at close range, judging from the powder burn. The killer wasted another four rounds in him as he lay face down on the town dump. That first shot killed him as dead as anyone can get."

"How do you know he was killed on the dump, Doc? Couldn't he have been gunned somewheres else and left there as an afterthought?"

"Do I question your professionalism, damn it? I'm the coroner here as well as the best mortician in Arizona. So, naturally, nobody moved the body until I got there. When we rolled it over to put it in the basket, the ground was still wet under his pants, and piss dries *fast* under the sun we have here. Since you're so smart, suppose you tell me what that had to mean, Deputy."

Longarm nodded. "A man killed instantly drains his bladder where he hits the ground. So he was led alive to the dump, willing or not, and killed right where he was found. Any notion how long he lay there first?"

"No more than an hour or so. He naturally never cooled under a noonday desert sun. But he would have been stiffer to stuff in the basket had he been there much longer."

Longarm turned to the town law to ask, "Just how public is this public dumping ground, pard?"

The other lawman said, "I follow your drift. But though it was broad daylight, you can't see the dump from any nearby houses, since nobody would build a house near such a stinky place. Another thing the killer or killers had going for 'em was the time of day. Nobody hauls garbage when it's that hot. He was found by accident by some loco Mex kids, hunting rats with slingshots. They run into town, scared skinny, and the rest you know."

Longarm doubted that, but he kept his voice polite as he asked, "Do you have the names of the kids as found this jasper? They might have noticed something out there aside from the body."

The local law looked sort of sheepish. "Hell, who keeps track of Mex names? They all sound the same to a white man. They was just a pair of bitty greasers. I'll know 'em if I see 'em around town again . . . I hope. Mex kids all look a lot alike, too."

Longarm nodded, keeping his disgust to himself, and turned back to the undertaker—coroner. "I'd like a look at a round or so you dug out of him, Doc," he said.

The older man frowned. "What are you talking about? I never probed for the damned bullets. Why should I have? I guess I know a bullethole when I see one, damn it. You've no idea how many of my customers come to me with bulletholes in 'em!"

"Yeah, but there's bullets and then there's bullets, Doc. As of the moment nobody can say for sure whether this gent was killed by a whore pistol or a man-sized dragoon. I might be able to make an educated guess, given at least one round to study some."

The undertaker swore under his breath, stepped over to the zinc table, and picked up a man-sized scalpel. Longarm sort of expected him to roll the corpse over to get at the back. But he simply slashed the dead man's denim shirt, sliced the waxy white flesh wide open, and reach into the innards of his chest like he was cleaning a chicken. He felt about in the squish, nodded, and pulled out a mighty messy hand with a wet slug grasped in his slippery fingers.

He held it out to Longarm, who managed not to gulp as the cold, wet lump dropped in his palm. The deputy who'd brought him wheezed and headed for the nearest door.

Longarm held the slightly deformed lead slug up to the light and said, "Forty-four-forty, like me and nine out of ten professional gunslicks use. Had to come from a sidearm, from what you said about powder burns. Had someone pumped the other rounds into him with a rifle, straight down, they wouldn't have entered him so cool."

The undertaker–coroner shrugged. "I may as well add that to my official report, then. But it still seems to me that almost anyone could have gunned him."

Longarm shook his head. "Not just anyone. Someone who had a reason. I don't recall this cadaver's face from any Wanted poster. But had he not been a stranger to Tucson, he'd have been given a name by now. So, if he was new to town, the man as killed him might have been new to town as well. Hardly anybody kills a total stranger just for practice."

The undertaker–coroner brightened as much as such a sober-looking cuss could manage and said, "By gum, that does let all the local boys off the hook, doesn't it?"

"Not hardly," Longarm said. "I said it seemed *likely* the dead man was a stranger. But it's still possible someone from Tucson knew this stranger better than the rest of you might have. You went through his pockets, of course?"

"Naturally. He was packing no identification. All we found in his pockets was a cheap jackknife, one broken match, and exactly five dollars and thirty-seven cents."

"Paper money or real money, Doc?"

"A five-dollar bank note, and the rest in change. Is there any point to *that* question, Deputy Long?"

"Maybe. Was the paper bill new, or old and waddy?"

"Good God, how should I know? Who worries about how old paper money is, as long as it's real? Wait a minute. Now that you mention it, the fiver *was* fairly crisp and clean. Not good as new, but . . . *What* in hell are we talking about, please?"

Longarm said, "A man who cashed a twenty-five-dollar bond at a bank would have been paid off in fresher than usual bank notes. A gang leader who's told him not to would be angry about it, too. But a kid this young might not have taken him serious. Five dollars left out of twenty-odd and change adds up to foolish spending when you consider how drunk your average cowhand can get in less'n a week on much less. So there's a fifty-fifty chance that what we has on ice here is a junior member of the gang I'm after, gunned by his confederates for unprofessional behavior."

The older man asked, "What do you mean, fifty-fifty? It looks to me as if you've hit the nail right on the head! Can I shove him back in now? The ice is starting to melt and ice is dear as hell in Tucson, even in the wintertime!"

Longarm nodded, but as the undertaker–coroner slid the remains out of view, Longarm said, "Don't mortgage your farm on my educated guesswork just yet, Doc. I could be right. But on the other hand, I could be wrong. You said yourself this was a tough old town and sometimes strangers do get shot just for practice, even in more civilized parts."

Chapter 3

The town lawman was waiting out front as Longarm left the undertaking establishment. He said, "Jesus, did you see how he just reached into that dead boy's guts without blinking an eye? I feared I was about to puke in there. You sure must have a strong stomach, Longarm."

Longarm shrugged. "I puked a lot early in the War. After Shiloh my stomach settled some. It had to. Unless a soldier keeps at least some of his food down, he just starves to death. But Doc's methods *are* a mite unsettling. So what say we go have a drink and get the green taste out of our mouths?"

The town lawman said that sounded like a swell notion and that the nearest saloon was catty-corner across the street. As they cut across, he added, "I didn't know you rode in the War, Longarm. Which side was you on?"

"I disremember," Longarm said. "The War ended fifteen years or so ago, and we was all young and foolish, on both sides. I'm more interested in here and now. Is this a tough saloon you're taking me to? I've a reason for asking."

"Hell, Longarm, nobody's about to tangle with a man of *your* rep! Not on this side of the tracks, leastways. Nobody with a lick of sense ever drinks in them greaser joints on the *wrong* side of the tracks."

Longarm made a mental note regarding the parts of town the local law didn't seem too interested in. He decided it might be more productive to visit there later, alone. Shady barkeeps and soiled doves hardly ever talked much to strangers in the company of a known badge-toter. That was one reason Longarm kept his own federal badge out of sight most of the time.

The saloon was set up like the Long Branch in Dodge, utilitarian, for serious drinkers. The bar ran the length of one wall, leaving a narrow space under the low pressed-tin ceiling for one row of tables, all taken at the moment. A door at the rear of the narrow layout was lettered PRIVATE. MEMBERS ONLY. Longarm didn't ask what went on in the back room. It was often disgusting, but hardly ever a federal matter.

They bellied up to the crowded bar. Longarm ordered Maryland rye and, when the barkeep said he'd never heard of it, settled for needled beer. It was hard to poison a man with rotgut diluted by beer and the nice thing about beer, west of the Big Muddy, was that if you could drink it at all it had to be safer than the local water. The town deputy ordered straight redeye. It was small wonder he was suffering stomach trouble.

Longarm meant to get rid of him as soon as he gracefully could. For one thing, the not-too-bright cuss was supposed to be on duty, no matter how good this excuse was. For another, had Longarm wanted another lawman backing his play he'd have brought along Deputy Guilfoyle, Flynn, or some other trained federal officer likely to act more predictable in a pinch. Longarm preferred to work alone because even a sidekick one could count on could be just an added worry at times. He figured he had enough on his plate just watching out for himself when times got rough, and it was easier to write reports to the department's liking when one didn't have another deputy calling one a big fibber.

Longarm had eased to his place at the bar as gently as possible, of course. Even if he hadn't, it seemed odd that the rough-looking young gent at his right elbow waited until he'd been served and had a full beer schooner in his gun hand before he said, "Watch who you're *shoving,* you cocksucker!"

Longarm froze in place but kept his voice as gentle as his smile as he replied softly, "Would you like to rephrase that remark, cowboy?"

The deputy on Longarm's left gasped, "Hold on, Laredo! You know me and I know you, but afore you calls the gent I'm drinking with a cocksucker, I'd best explain who he really is!"

Laredo said, "Don't care who he is. He was rude as hell to my elbow just now and he who touches my elbow must die, or say he's sorry, sudden as hell!"

"I'm sorry, Laredo," Longarm said. "For we're both too young to die and, seeing you're a pal of my pal, here, we'll just say no more about it, hear?"

Others were moving away from the bar now, leaving plenty of room for Laredo. But he chose not to take advantage of it as he kept crowding Longarm, saying, "Shit, he ain't no pal of mine. He's just *yellow.* Ain't that right, you yellow-livered little mother-fucker?"

The town deputy said, "Aw, Laredo, that ain't no way to talk."

Laredo asked sarcastically, "Why, is there ladies present? I don't see no gals in here, unless I counts a copper badge who squats to piss as less than a man!"

The deputy paled, but did nothing.

32

"Is this a long-established feud between you gents, or can anybody get in?" Longarm asked quietly.

Laredo eyed Longarm with renewed interest. "We ain't at feud right now," he said. "It's a long-established fact of life that the local law is scared of me. But if *you'd* like to dance, just call the tune and I'll do my best to follow you."

The deputy behind Longarm gasped. "Damn it, Laredo, I know you're crazy when you're drunk, but the man's called *Longarm!*"

The name didn't seem to mean anything to Laredo, but an older and wiser man in the crowd sighed, "Oh, my God, let me out of here, boys! *This* one's gonna be for *real!*"

A couple of others had apparently heard of Longarm, too, while those who hadn't seemed willing to take the advice of their elders. So in no time at all Longarm and the town bully seemed to have the saloon all to themselves. The barkeep had grabbed the mirror and hit the floor, while even the deputy who had told him the place was all right had joined the stampede out the door.

Longarm chuckled, still holding his barely tasted beer schooner in his gun hand as he said, "It's just as well we have this chance to talk in private, Laredo. For you look like a nice young gent, and I understand the position you've blundered your way into."

Laredo stepped away from the bar just enough to clear his side-draw .45 for action. "What are you talking about?" he asked. "Do you have the sand in your craw for a fight, or are you all mouth, like most?"

Longarm said, "Laredo, you are suffering a grave misconception about the way life works. I can see you've been drinking pretty good and I suspicion you've been reading Ned Buntline's Wild West magazines and not getting the joke. I ain't impressed with your wild and woolly bullshit because, for one thing, I'm a full-grown man. The reason *other* full-grown men you've pulled this shit on have let

33

you live, up to now, is that anyone but an asshole kid can see that even when you *win* a pointless fight, it can spoil the rest of the evening for you. Men with wives or gals waiting for 'em at home will put up with a surprising amount of guff from a mean drunk. But it ain't because they're *scared*. It's because hardly anyone would ever get home regular if he fought every asshole he met up with in this asshole world."

"Who are you calling an asshole? *Draw,* you cock-sucker!"

"Now, sonny, you know damned well I'm holding this schooner in my gun hand while you jaw so silly. It's tempting as hell to put this beer down or toss it in your face, just to see how sudden you can get more neighborly. But I'm more neighborly than the man you'll surely meet up with sooner or later if you don't mend your ways. So I'll tell you what we'd best do. We'd best pretend for the public at large that after some discussion we agreed to kiss and make up. That way, you won't make *me* look bad and I won't make *you* look bad, see?"

Laredo stared at the beer schooner between them, his red eyes filled with the dull cunning of the natural bully, and asked, "Hey, what makes you so brave? Can't you see there's no way in hell you could get to your gun, cross draw, without putting that schooner down first?"

Longarm smiled thinly. "I've been using it to hold your attention, Laredo, the way a snake in a tree freezes a little birdie. Stage magicians call it misdirection, but it works in situations like this as well. You've been dead since you first started up with me. But I feel so sorry for you that I aim to show you a trade secret. You see this other hand I got here, dangling off the edge of the bar as I rest my elbow so casual? Don't do nothing silly. Just watch."

He turned his free left hand over, revealing the double-barrel derringer he'd been holding, palmed, on the bully all this time. As Laredo's jaw dropped, Longarm said, "I shoot left-handed almost as well, and you've been standing there flapping your mouth at point-blank range for even a *poor* shot. So are we going to be pals after all, or are you just too damned dumb to go on breathing air more sensible folks could use?"

Laredo gulped and said, "Well, since you put it that way, I'd be proud to drink with you, Longarm. I'm buying, of course."

"I know," Longarm said, then called out in a louder tone, "Hey, barkeep? You can come up now. War's over."

The barkeep raised a cautious head from down at the far end of the bar, sighed with relief, and got to his feet to join them, still looking nervous. Laredo said he wanted his usual and as the barkeep poured the double shot for him Longarm could see why the kid's mental stability was in such poor shape. But drinking oneself to an early grave wasn't a federal offense, so Longarm just sipped his beer without comment.

Laredo swallowed his redeye neat, in one gulp, and slammed the shotglass down with a wheeze. "That's what I needed more'n a fight, anyway," he said. "I've heard the name Longarm somewheres before. But I just can't connect it up to any gunslick I've ever admired."

"I didn't think you could have," Longarm said. "But since you're the local authority on gunslicks, Laredo, I'd sure like to hear about any such gents here in Tucson."

Laredo signaled for another drink. "Ain't *nobody* as tough as me in Tucson," he growled. "I'm so mean I curdles milk in the cow just looking over the fence at her. I don't want to fight with *you* no more. But if there's *another* cocksucker in town who thinks he's as good as me, just point him out and we'll see about that, hear?"

"Do you know anything about that kid they found shot this afternoon on the city dump, Laredo?"

"Nope. Heard about it, though. They say he was shot in the back. Do I look like a piss-ant who'd shoot a man in the back?"

He looked more like a drunk who was about to fall on his face to Longarm. But the tall deputy said, "Not hardly. A gent with your habit of calling total strangers cocksuckers would likely know if there was anyone new in town given to sudden surly displays of gunplay, right?"

"What? Sure, hell, there ain't a man packing a gun in Tucson I ain't calt a cocksucker at least once. Why do you ask?"

"They've either ridden on or they're as cool as I figured real pros would be," said Longarm, half to himself.

Laredo didn't answer. He suddenly just let go of the bar and was falling over backwards as if someone had chopped him off at the ankles. Longarm could have stopped him, but he saw no reason to, so he didn't. As Laredo hit the sawdust-covered planking with a pleasant-sounding thump, Longarm asked the barkeep, "Does he do that often?"

The barkeep sighed and said, "At least twice a week. Thanks for not killing him, Longarm. I mostly ducked because I heard about you when I was working in Cheyenne. You're a real gent, like the boys all said."

"I'm here on more important matters. You must have heard enough just now to know I'm interested in *real* gunslicks. A bunch of say a dozen, or eleven, if I'm right about that corpse on ice across the way. You'd recall if you'd noticed that many strangers in a bunch, wouldn't you?"

The barkeep nodded, but said, "The county sheriff and other federal deps has already asked me that same question, Longarm. If there's a fair-sized gang sticking together here in Tucson, they ain't been doing so here along the main street."

"How about the less seemly parts of town, across the tracks?"

36

"Lord, nobody *white* goes over to Mex Town after dark, Longarm. Are we talking about a white gang or Mex banditos?"

"The description has 'em down as white, albeit wearing masks and yellow slickers while they rob banks, of course. I've been in some tough old Mex Towns, and I've noticed there's usually a few gringo residents. Most trouble our kind has with 'em is caused by the lingo barrier, and I can talk a little Border Mex if I have to."

The barkeep shook his head. "Don't go there till broad day, with an armed escort, Longarm. We ain't talking about *ordinary* greasers. So it don't matter if you can talk to them or not. They never *listen* when they get a crack at a white man alone in their territory!"

The first thing Longarm noticed about the so-called Mexican quarter of Tucson was that it was over twice as big as the English-speaking area. So the folks running the whole place saved a bundle on street lighting, trash collecting, and such. City planning wasn't an advanced art anywhere this far west, but the narrow, twisty lanes between the casually constructed adobe houses and garden walls would have made for some confusion even for a stranger to the neighborhood who could see where he was going. The desert stars above were brighter than most, of course, but the moon had set, and even bright stars left a lot to be desired in the way of illumination. So Longarm had to feel his way along the mud bricks to his left as he tried to home in on the distant twanging of a Spanish git-fiddle. Music usually meant activity. Spanish-speaking folk didn't sing in bed any more than anyone else did.

Longarm rounded a corner, expecting to see some glimmer at least of not-too-distant light, since that was where the twanging seemed to be coming from. But, if anything, the way ahead was even darker. It was hard to tell, since it was pitch-black between the close-set walls no matter where a man might be in this infernal maze.

He was moving slowly, left hand leading the way toward the sound of music, when he heard something less pleasant in the dark ahead and froze, sensing that he might have made a tactical error back at that corner.

He couldn't see a thing as he stared soberly in the direction of the Winchester or Henry he'd just heard cocked. He silently drew his own .44-40, in case he was wrong. Then he said, "Hold your fire, El Gato. We used to be pals. It's my sincere hope we still are."

A familiar voice replied cautiously, *"Madre de Dios!* Is that you, Longarm? *En verdad,* you must see better than me in the dark if you recognize me at this range!"

Longarm chuckled as he put his gun away. "Nobody sees as well as the gent they call The Cat, in the dark or broad daylight. That's how I knew it had to be you. What are you doing this far north of the border, El Gato?"

The still invisible Mexican bandit or, as he preferred to be called, rebel, moved closer, saying, "I am surprised for to meet you here, too. May I hope the agreement we made over in Chihuahua still stands, *amigo?"*

Longarm said, "Don't see why not, as long as it's understood the only folks you shoot are Rurales, Federales, and such. Or that the only banks you rob are in Diaz's jurisdiction. For, as I told you when we last met, south of the border, *El Presidente* Diaz don't seem to recognize either my badge or my right to live."

He could see El Gato now, sort of. Had not Longarm had better night vision than most men, with the exception of freaks like he was talking to, he wouldn't even have been able to make out the big sombrero or the saddle gun now politely down at El Gato's side. The Mexican laughed boyishly and said, *"Bueno.* If my enemies are still your enemies, you are still my friend. For why are you here in the

Mexican quarter at midnight, Longarm? Some of the people a gringo could meet here at this hour do not share my feelings toward your kind, you know."

"Someone was just saying that to me, in a saloon where *your* kind might not feel comfortable," Longarm replied. "But I was hoping to meet up with someone reasonable and, what do you know, I just did."

El Gato shifted his Henry to his left hand and held out his gun hand to shake on it. "You always have been too lucky for to believe," he said. "But now that you are here, with me for to back your play, what are we talking about? Not even a madman of your *raza* could be in this part of Tucson at midnight for to eat a woman or kiss a chili pepper, eh?"

Longarm said, "I'm here on duty. I'd best warn you up front I'm on the trail of bank robbers. I sure hope you haven't been robbing any banks north of the border, old son."

El Gato chuckled and said, "That last bank I robbed was in Magdalena, en la Estada de Sonora. For some reason, los Rurales were not amused. So I felt it prudent for to visit your more friendly country for a time. You have my word my *muchachos* and me have not been naughty up here in Arizona. We wish for to keep Los Estados Unidos a friendly place for to visit, eh?"

"Your word's always been good enough for me, El Gato," Longarm said. "Is there someplace where we can sit down to talk? I've reason to suspicion at least one old gringo boy who wasn't as good a citizen of these United States as you and your boys might have been playing big spender with the gals in this part of town."

El Gato took his arm and they were able to move faster, thanks to his uncanny eyes, as he led Longarm to an invisible door in a pitch-black alley and, once it was open, into a candle-lit cantina filled with a crowd of Mexicans and at least a few Indians, unless head-bands and long hair were the current fashion in this part of Tucson.

A sad, skinny gent was strumming the guitar Longarm had heard, one foot on a chair as he sang in a soft falsetto about some gypsy killing himself for the love of a high-born señorita who never noticed. Longarm was braced for the growling a gringo usually heard when he entered such an establishment, but nobody did. It wasn't safe to growl anywhere near El Gato unless one had serious intent of slapping leather. The young bandit was almost girlishly handsome and his black leather charro outfit and silver-laced black sombrero might have seemed sissy in Dodge. But nobody with a lick of sense ever laughed at El Gato, even when they didn't know his name. He wasn't called The Cat just for seeing in the dark like a cat. He moved with the sinister grace of a black panther and the grips of his matched .45s were oversized and carved tailor-made to fit his not at all artistic hands.

El Gato headed for a blue-painted table in a corner as Longarm followed. The gents who had likely thought it was their table up to now hastily got up, smiling, to offer their chairs. Longarm noticed that El Gato thanked them courteously. He couldn't help wondering what would have happened if they hadn't offered.

Longarm and his gracious host were barely seated before a plump but pretty cantina girl dashed over to them with a tray bearing lemons, a salt cellar, a knife, and a bottle of tequila, still sealed, with the worm still floating in it. Longarm didn't make the usual gringo comment about the cactus worm as El Gato opened the bottle. He knew it was the sign of good stuff, dropped in the bottle to show it was real cactus juice.

El Gato passed him the bottle first. Longarm sprinkled salt on the back of his hand, licked it, and took a polite belt of tequila. He managed not to gasp as he handed it to the bandit, who had meanwhile been slicing lemons. El Gato asked, "Don't you need for to suck lemon, after your tequila? Most men do."

Longarm held back his tears by sheer will power as he said, "Naw, good stuff ain't that hard to take. I only need the lemon when I don't see the worm."

So, naturally, El Gato had to take his own belt without the lemon. He never blinked an eye as he put the bottle down, observing, "You are right, it is very mild. Almost as mild as the stuff they make for you Yanquis, back home. Do you think it could be watered? It bears the label of a most respected firm."

"Oh, I'm sure it's just mellowed with age. That critter slopping about in it looks sort of wrinkled. Could we talk about my less pleasant reasons for coming over here tonight, El Gato?"

The Mexican nodded, so Longarm was able to bring him up to date without having to swallow more than another two slugs of tequila in the process.

El Gato had another belt to consider the matter, then he said, "A gringo spending twenty dollars on two-bit *putas* in less than a week would cause a certain amount of gossip among the soiled doves of the area. But I am the liberator of Mexico, not a pimp. I am also, like you, a stranger to many of the people of my *raza*, this far north of the border. I shall have to contact members of the local power structure for you. But first let us go over that part about the *real dinero* your own gringo bandits rode off with. Twenty thousand, divided among say ten riders, comes to more than a thousand for each, in cash. So for why would your mysterious corpse have needed for to cash one of those stolen bearer bonds so *soon?*"

Longarm said, "I've been pondering that myself. Even allowing for mighty foolish spending, the Maricopa job wasn't that long ago, and a raggedy kid dressed cow should have become famous spending *that* much! I can see a couple

41

of ways it might work, sort of. Like I said, he was young, and he couldn't have been in the bank robbing trade that long, since there'd be paper out on him if he had. So he might have been riding as a sort of underpaid apprentice. The gang leader likely took half or more of the loot as his own fair share, and—"

"You call that fair?" El Gato cut in with a frown.

Longarm shushed him. "You wouldn't share that way and I wouldn't share that way, but some crooks are a mite crooked-minded, seeing as most get started stealing from friends and kin to begin with. If the leader took half or more, even his full partners got say five or six hundred apiece in cash, and mayhaps a few thousand in harder-to-cash bonds."

El Gato nodded, but objected, "Even a man spending five hundred in just a few weeks should have left a trail of people who would remember him, no?"

"That's why I'm looking for folks who remember him. I can't see even a born Fagin paying off that kid in pure air, and it would have been dumb for a pro to give him even one of them bonds." He took a thoughtful sip of tequila and added, "I got to send me some wires, come morning. The reports my office gave me never mentioned whether the cash they took from the Maricopa bank was paper or heavy metal."

"Ah, you think they may have buried much of the real *dinero* for to ride faster?"

"Well, they sure as hell rode faster than any posse. But there's still something fishy about the whole thing. To get away so slick, and to stay got-away so good with so many people looking for 'em, the gang or at least its leader has to be smarter than average. I hardly ever rob banks, yet I'm smart enough to see that if I was going to the trouble of hiding any part of the loot I'd be hiding the hot bonds first and keeping at least some untraceable spending money, even in the form of heavy silver dollars."

"*Si*, but the boy who cashed that bond here in Tucson was not smart, and that is for why his *compañeros* had to kill him, no?"

Longarm shrugged and said, "I can't come up with nothing better. But he must have been over the edge from dumb to just plain loco, unless he had a mighty good reason for needing money. And, you're right, they wouldn't have given him a share of the bonds without giving him at least a few bucks."

"I shall go for to see what I can find out," El Gato said. "Where can I find you as soon as I know anything?"

Longarm frowned and replied, "I ain't sure. I haven't had time to find a hotel room here in Tucson yet."

"You got a room. Upstairs. That way I will not have to fight my way to you in the less friendly part of town." El Gato saw Longarm's look of hesitation and asked, "What is wrong? Are you too proud for to spend the night in a greaser *posada?*"

"Hell, a man who's slept in the prairie in winter can sleep anywheres. It's just that my things is still checked at the railroad depot, and I was told they might not be safe there."

"You got your things. Give me your claim check and I will send someone for to bring them here to you."

Longarm handed El Gato his claim check and a quarter to tip the baggage smasher. The Mexican snapped his fingers as he put the check away for now. The plump cantina girl came over and El Gato told her, in Spanish Longarm was able to follow, "This man is my friend. He shall be staying here tonight, in a clean bed, in a room with no bugs. If you do not take good care of him, I shall burn the place down. If you make him most comfortable, you may put the cost on my bill, eh?"

The girl seemed to think that could be arranged. Both men rose and El Gato left by the front door as Longarm followed the girl and the tequila bottle upstairs.

She took a candle from a wall sconce at the head of the stairs and led him to a corner room which had cross-ventilation, if one wanted to open the shutters of the two narrow windows set in the thick adobe walls. The bed was a mattress on the floor against one wall. The bedding consisted of homespun cotton sheeting with corn-husk pillows and a Navajo blanket folded neatly at the foot of the mattress in the unlikely event it ever cooled off enough to matter. The girl set the candlestick on the wide stucco sill of one window and turned to ask, *"Es rudo, pero limpio, no?"*

He said, *"Si, hable Ingles?"*

She fluttered her lashes and replied, "Only a leetle, *señor*. We do not have many Anglos staying here. I am called Gordita."

He said she could call him Custis and resisted the impulse to tell her she wasn't all that fat. For Gordita wasn't a proper gal's name in Spanish. It meant something like "Chubby" and, in simple truth, it fit her. Still, by gentle candlelight— or perhaps because he'd had such a long, lonesome train ride—she looked a mite better up here than she had downstairs serving drinks.

Gordita must have been about seventeen to twenty, certainly no more. For gals with her build figured to be just plain fat before they made twenty-five. From the color of her smooth brown skin and the way her almond eyes were set in her little round skull, she had to have more Indian than Spanish blood in her. Likely she was Papago or Pima. Desert Indians tended to be skinny as hell in the desert, but because they were used to getting by on so little, they tended to blow up like balloons when they started to eat like Americans or Mexicans. But, so far, little Gordita was still closer to being pleasantly plump than outright fat.

He wondered how come she was still hanging about, having shown him the little there was to see in these Spartan quarters. He knew *posada* help weren't used to being tipped for every service. A gent was supposed to take care of them when he checked out. But he was tired, and she didn't look like a good conversationalist, so he reached in his pants for a dime.

When he held it out to her Gordita gasped and insisted, *"Pero no!* Do you take me for a *puta,* Señor Custis? You are here as a *guest,* not a mere customer!"

He said he was sorry as hell and put the coin away. Then he hung his hat, frock coat, and gun rig on the pegs provided along the adobe wall in hopes she would see that he meant to turn in. But when he turned around she was not only still standing there, she was taking off her own duds.

As he watched, bemused, Gordita dropped her circle skirt around her bare feet, pulled her frilly cotton blouse off over her head, and left them where they'd fallen to step over to the mattress. She dropped to her plump knees, made the Sign of the Cross across her firm, bare muskmelon breasts, and slid her plump, bare ass between the sheets.

He didn't know what to say, so he didn't say anything as he took off his vest and got to work on the buttons of his hickory shirt.

Gordita looked up shyly and asked, "Could we have the candle out, *por favor?* I have always been a leetle shy weeth men."

He laughed like hell and moved over to the window to snuff the candle as, behind him in the dark, Gordita pleaded, "Do not make fun of me! I try for to watch my weight, but working around the smell of food all day is most hard on a girl's figure."

He said he wasn't laughing at her, exactly, as he opened the window shutters to have at least some air if not light on the subject. Then he finished dressing and did what any other man who didn't want to be called a sissy would have. He got between the rough sheeting with the little gal and took her in his arms.

As he did so, Gordita hugged him back with her smooth, plump arms but almost whimpered, "Be gentle weeth me, *por favor*. I am not used to sleeping with guests here and, in truth, you are so beeg you frighten me a leetle!"

He frowned thoughtfully. "Hold on. We'd best study on just what's going on here. Are you saying going to bed with me wasn't your own exact notion, Gordita?" he asked.

"I was ordered for to take good care of you, no?" she replied, as she shyly reached down to take the matter firmly in hand. Then, as her plump but short fingers curled around his growing desire, she gasped, *"Madre de Dios!* I knew you were beeg, but not *thees* beeg!"

He knew his pecker would never forgive him, but he still had to say, "You'd best let go, if you don't really want to, Gordita."

"Do you not want me?"

"You'd be in position to know I was lying, now, if I said I didn't. But it ain't my style to take advantage of a woman against her will. So if you was only following El Gato's orders, getting us both in this embarrassing position, it ain't too late for us to get out of it. But it will be, mighty soon, if you don't let go my privates!"

She snuggled closer and commenced to stroke his shaft to full attention as she replied, *"Ay, que romantico!* You are most gallant as well as most good lookeeng, Coostees. I confess I was a leetle annoyed when El Gato told me he would burn us out unless I acted the part of a weekend woman for you, *pero . . ."*

"Hold on," he cut in, running his own free hand along her smooth warm curves. "My Spanish ain't that bad, and I was there. El Gato never said anything about you being *this* friendly. He just said he expected you to treat me right."

46

She giggled and said, *"Sí,* but eet ees better for to take a heent from El Gato to the leemit rather than to have heem angry. Are you a *bandito,* too, Coostees?"

"Not exactly. Me and old El Gato got to be pals in Chihuahua a spell back, with the same folk gunning for us both. It's true El Gato is a bandit, and a surly one at that, but we was forced to agree that no man shooting at los Rurales can be all bad, so . . ."

He saw she wasn't interested in the rest of his story, so he stopped and just lay back to enjoy it as Gordita slid all the way down and proceeded to inhale on his *cigaro* with considerable skill for a gal who said she didn't do this sort of thing too often.

But a man who'd been frustrated by a redhead on the Denver & Rio Grande and ridden the rest of the way lonesome didn't need the stimulation of a French lesson from a Mexican gal as much as he needed the real thing. So he sat up, grabbed her bobbing head, and placed it firmly on the folded Navajo blanket as he mounted her right, or tried to.

Gordita held her plump thighs together, protesting, "Not that way! You are too beeg for me, *querido!"*

But he didn't need further flattery to stimulate his raging erection, and she'd carried this situation past maidenly shyness into just plain silly. So he forced her chubby thighs apart, rolled into the well-padded saddle between, and proceeded to do what comes naturally as she sighed, "Oh, you are so masterful!"

She was built sort of small as well as hot between the legs, despite the width of her considerable hips. So he didn't object when she raised her plump knees and braced them close together against his bare chest, saying, "Oh, *que linda,* you can move as fast as you like, now. As long as you don't heet bottom weeth every stroke, eh?"

That sounded fair. So he proceeded to make up for that long, dull train trip with considerable enthusiasm. He naturally climaxed fast the first time, but long before he eja-culated in her Gordita had stopped fretting about how big he was and had her bare heels hooked against his collar bones to take it as deep as it could go, moaning and groaning in Spanish as she rolled her head back and forth on the blanket, begging for at least another yard of him as she bounced her well-padded rump to meet every stroke. So by the time they'd come together they were old friends indeed, and when he rolled off to catch his second wind the plump little spitfire was on top of him, bouncing like a rubber ball with his semi-sated shaft in her, lest it go soft before he could forget how much he loved her, she said.

It was amazing to consider that he'd sort of dismissed her as a little brown butterball at first sight, downstairs. For up here in the dark he couldn't think of a thing about her a man with a lick of sense would want to change. When he got on top again, this time with her head rolling all over a crunchy corn-husk pillow, he was pleased as punch about her considerable dusky rump. For it would have been sort of distracting to have corn-husks crunching under his nuts, had they needed a pillow under her. But, thanks to the handy way she was built, Gordita without a pillow under her pre-sented an angle most gals would have needed *two* pillows to manage and, as he hit bottom with every stroke, she hugged him with her loving legs and begged for it harder and deeper, coming over and over ahead of him. So he tended to believe she hadn't been doing this too often in recent memory and so, when they stopped to share a smoke and catch their wind again, he didn't object too much when Gordita suggested they quit fooling around and get really down and dirty.

Chapter 4

When Longarm woke up the next morning he was alone on the mattress, but El Gato was hunkered over him. The bandit asked if he'd had a pleasant night. Longarm propped himself up on one elbow, rubbed his face, and muttered, "I'll get you for that, you sneaky rascal. But, speaking of sneaking, what else did you fix me up with last night?"

El Gato said, "Your gear is downstairs, behind the bar. It was the best we could do. If there is a pimp or slut in the Mexican quarter I did not speak to, I do not wish for to meet anyone less unashamed. I was not able to get a line on your young bandit who spent money so freely in the last few days. He did not spend it in this part of town. Few of the *putas* entertain your kind, and those they do, including two lawmen and a preacher, are well known to them."

"Never mind about the infernal *regulars*. Couldn't they be confused about the dead boy's age? No offense, but some of your people tend to look small and youthsome, full-growed. The body in the box of ice was taller than most

Mexican *mestizos* and, to a gal used to runtier gents, he might have looked older."

El Gato, who was taller than many an Anglo and pure Spanish enough to pass for one if he didn't dress so funny, shrugged and said, "I thought of that. But they told me they have not been fucked by any gringo cowhand since the spring roundup. You must understand that this time of the year makes for slow business even over on the main streets of Tucson, Longarm."

"I understand it. But that's not saying I *like* it. For I seem to have risked my ass in this part of town for nothing."

El Gato smiled softly at the spotted and rumpled sheets. "I am sorry you spent such an uncomfortable night. I shall have a *chico* carry your things to grander surroundings for you, eh?"

Longarm grinned sheepishly and said, "Hold the thought. I can't think of a better base of operation while I'm here in Tucson. For one thing, any members of the American gang would be expecting me to check into a hotel closer to the depot. You're going to have to let me pay the folk here at this posada, though. I know you ain't used to paying for nothing, since Robin Hood was one of our boys. But I don't feel right imposing."

El Gato scowled and demanded, "Did that *puta* ask for money? Did she *dare?*"

"Now, don't get your bowels in an uproar, and don't call a pal of mine no *puta,*" Longarm said. "So far, I ain't spent a dime on anything here. But before I leave I mean to lay some silver on 'em, and you can go to hell if you don't like it. What's the going rate for this here room?"

"Two bits a night, *Americano.* It's the best *posada* in the district. But I have already paid them. You see, I *do* know about Robin Hood."

"I was wondering how come nobody ever turned you in. All right, I know you won't take my money, so I'll owe it

50

to you in drinks. Right now I got to get back over to the main street and send me some wires and such. Before we part friendly, I may need a horse, and the livery over by the depot may be more public than I'd like."

El Gato nodded. "What kind of a mount? Fast or long-winded?"

Longarm thought and said, "It's too hot to ride sudden. Too hot to ride slow and steady across that furnace floor outside, come to study on it. You ride across deserts more than I do, El Gato. What would you suggest for a man just poking about, not knowing exactly where he's going?"

"A Spanish mule would carry you farther than any horse with the water so far apart. But I know how you *Americanos* feel about being seen on a mere mule."

"There you go putting your own thoughts in another man's head," sighed Longarm. "I once found a *pair* of mules handy as hell in the hot canyons of the Four Corners Country. So a good riding mule might be just the ticket. What would the hire of one cost me?"

El Gato laughed. "Do not be ridiculous. I am a professional liberator of Mexico, not a dealer in livestock."

"You mean you never *sells* the horses, pigs, and chickens you and your boys steal every chance you get?"

El Gato laughed and said, "When you are ready for to ride out, you will find your mount waiting in the stable out back. That is a whole bottle of tequila, *good* tequila, you will owe me, now."

They shook on it, and El Gato left. Longarm saw that Gordita had left a basin of water and some clean cotton rags for him on the floor in one corner. He gave himself a whore bath and got dressed and gunned.

Downstairs, there was nobody in the cantina at this hour except an old man swabbing the floor. Longarm nodded to him and went outside. It felt like stepping into a furnace, and it wasn't anywhere near noon yet. He took off his coat and carried it over his left arm. Folks in Arizona Territory didn't stare as much at openly worn sidearms as the prissier townees of Denver.

Getting back to the main part of town with the sun beating him over the head seemed to take longer than crossing the tracks by starlight had. It was cooler in the Western Union office by the depot. He told the clerk on duty who he was and, sure enough, a wire from the Denver office was waiting for him. So he opened it, read it, and swore some.

Another of the stolen bonds had been cashed in Nogales, on the border, sixty-odd miles due south. It got worse. A Mexican bank in Chihuahua had just demanded the face value less two percent for five thousand U. S. dollars for the paper they were holding. So the last of Billy Vail's message read:

THAT TIES IT STOP THEY MADE IT OVER THE LINE STOP TAKE NEXT TRAIN BACK STOP DUTCH CLEARED BY CJ STOP VAIL

Longarm picked up a telegram blank and a handy pencil to send back:

NO IT DONT STOP IT MEANS ONE AT LEAST MADE IT BUT 5000 IS ONLY ONE SHARE SO WHERES THE REST QUESTION MARK AND ITS MURDER ONE NOW DUE TO CORPSE WAITING FOR ME HERE STOP CONTINUING INVESTI-GATION STOP LONG

He told the clerk to send it at night-letter rates, since it would only upset old Billy to get it before he'd had a good night's sleep. Then he asked the local man, "If I aimed to get to Nogales in a hurry, could I catch a train, or do I really have to ride in that sun outside?"

The Western Union man smiled and said, "There's a spur line running down to pick up the ore they mine in Nogales, Deputy. Only runs twice a week, but you're in luck. They're making up the way-freight this very minute, over to the SP yards."

Longarm said, "Do tell? How soon could I get back by train, if Nogales turns up tedious on me?"

The clerk shrugged. "Next Monday, of course. I just said it only run twice a week. You'd best hurry if you aim to grab a ride."

Longarm shook his head. "No, thanks. I can't see being stuck for three days with nothing to do in a town I don't know anyone in. I could likely hire a strange mount and saddle down in Nogales to ride back sooner, but sixty-odd miles across your considerably sun-baked desert would be a mite tedious, even if I knew for sure I had a reason for doing such a fool chore. There's got to be a better way."

He went outside and crossed the dusty street to a beanery he'd noted in his recent travels. He went in and, since it wasn't a good idea to eat heavy in hot weather, only ordered steak and eggs for breakfast.

As he sat at the counter consuming the same, an older gent with a brass badge came in, studied Longarm some, and said, "I'm Marshal Cunningham. If you're Longarm, I've been looking for you. If you ain't, you're in trouble. For we have a city ordinance pertaining to that hardware on your left hip."

Longarm smiled and said, "I'm him. Do you want to see my badge and I.D.?"

Cunningham looked relieved, sat down beside him, and said, "If you know you carry a badge you must know who you are, Longarm. We just found out who that gent in the box used to be. Showed his picture around town and a cowhand recognized it. In life he answered to the handle of Bucky Bronson. He rode for the Double B, a horse

53

breeding outfit up the Santa Cruz about an hour's ride outten town. They're new to the territory and the boy must have lived sedate up until recent. None of the other folk in town recall him worth mention. But the hand as did says he bought a cow pony off the Double B a week or so ago and recalls the kid as decent enough to talk horseflesh with. We're fixing to send someone out to the Double B and see if they want to claim the remains."

Longarm washed down the last of his steak with black coffee. "I'd be proud to handle the chore for you, Marshal," he said. "Might kill more than one bird with one rock if I was to break the news to 'em gentle."

Cunningham nodded. "I figured you might like to ask some personal questions about the late Bucky Bronson. That's why I thought to have this discussion with you first. By the way, is it true Logan steered you into a tight spot and then punked out on you last night?"

Longarm didn't ask who Logan might be. The useless copper badge they had under discussion had to have some damned name or other. But he didn't want to cause trouble for a man who likely couldn't get a better job. So he just looked innocent and asked, "What tight spot are we talking about? So far most of the folk I've met in Tucson has treated me decent enough, Marshal."

"Bullshit," Cunningham said. "It's all over town how you knocked Laredo O'Hanlon on his ass when he had the drop on you. How come you didn't gun Laredo when you had the chance, and how come my deputy never saw fit to back a fellow lawman in trouble?"

Longarm laughed easily and said, "Hell, nobody needed backing. Old Laredo just fell down all by himself. As to your deputy, I'd called him away from duty at your lockup and he likely thought it was time he got back. He left before Laredo fell down and, like I said, there wasn't no real trouble."

Cunningham smiled thinly. "I admire a man who don't like to gossip. But it's still all over town that you kicked the shit outten the town bully, and if I was you I'd keep an eye out ahint me. You may or may not consider Laredo dangerous. But they call him Laredo because he had to leave Texas sudden, after a similar saloon incident. By now he's sober, and likely somewhat put out by the talk in town about you putting him on the floor, no matter how he got there. So, like I said, watch your back."

Longarm said, "I always do. How come the critter's allowed to run so loose if he's so ornery? You just said you had a city ordinance against packing hardware on the streets, and I couldn't help noticing old Laredo favors a straight-draw rig."

Cunningham looked away and murmured, "I'll surely arrest him the first time he really kills somebody. But he's got friends in high places and a permit for that gun. When he ain't getting drunk, he's a hired bodyguard for a big-shot banker here in town."

Longarm shrugged. "Must be why nobody robbed any banks here in Tucson, then." He started to mention the stolen bond cashed at the bank in Nogales, but decided not to. A lawman who allowed an idiot to run loose rawhiding the folks he was supposed to be protecting wasn't Longarm's idea of a serious peace officer, and *somebody* around here had to be covering up for that owlhoot gang he was interested in.

He asked Cunningham for further directions to the Double B spread. Then they shook on it outside and Longarm headed back to the Mexican quarter to get someone else to do his walking for him.

This time Gordita was alone in the cantina. She blushed when he came in and asked in what way she could be of service to a guest of El Gato.

He gave her a friendly kiss and an even friendlier pat on

55

her plump behind and told her they'd study on it later, in the cool of evening. Then he got his saddle gear from behind the bar and carried them out to the stable.

Sure enough, a cordovan Spanish mule was standing proud among the nondescript ponies in the stalls. The mule was two hands taller than the average cow pony, and he could see the horseflesh in its family tree was Arab. He didn't get any argument when he cinched his McClellan saddle on the big brute's back, and the critter opened its jaws for the bit like a kid who hadn't learned about dentists yet. He told it, "You wouldn't be frisking for a ride in the country, so, if you knew how hot it was outside. But you look like a good old mule. So we ought to get along tolerable."

It was doubtful the mule was used to being addressed in English, but it seemed to find Longarm's voice assuring. So it wasn't until Longarm had led it outside and mounted up that he found the mule was feeling friskier than the situation called for. As they bucked down the alley, Longarm cursed El Gato. But as they bounced out into the full glare of the noonday sun at the end of the alley, the mule winced its eyes half shut and settled into a comfortable frisky trot. Longarm forgave El Gato, for few horses could have taken the dry heat so easily. They headed for the nearby waters of the Santa Cruz and by the time they were moving upstream along the grassy banks of the shallow braided stream, the mule didn't argue when he reined it to a walk. It was hard to tell if the heat was sweating either of them. The bone-dry, thirsty air sucked sweat away as fast as it could come out. Longarm considered putting on the coat he'd lashed to the possibles roll behind him. He knew there were just two ways of dressing in desert country. It was safe to go bare like a Digger Indian or covered entirely with loose, floppy duds, like an Arab or Apache. In between was just asking for heatstroke. But he wasn't tanned as much as a desert Indian and just thinking about that tobacco tweed frock coat over his shirtsleeves hurt like hell. So he decided to go with just the shirt and vest for now.

They rode for half an hour with the brush and reeds of the riverside to one side and the crueler parts of Arizona in high summer on the other. Longarm had been ambushed often enough to stare thoughtfully at the bigger patches of prickly pear they passed. It hardly seemed likely that anyone but a total fool would be hiding behind any of the tall saguaros growing all around with their arms held up like someone had the drop on them. He didn't see any of them in fruit. The less tasty prickly pears had all been picked over, too. So he lit a smoke. The dry air made his mouth taste awful, but he wasn't thirsty inside, yet, and sipping every few minutes at warm canteen water could mess up a man's innards.

But by now his mount could likely use some water. So he reined into the shallow Santa Cruz and, as the mule lowered its head to have some muddy refreshment, Longarm looked back the way they'd just come. He could still see the railroad water tower of Tucson doing the shimmy in the shimmering desert air, but was it his imagination or had a blur about the size of a horse and rider shimmied behind that distant clump of pear or not?

He waited until he thought the mule had had enough for now and cranked its head up, telling it, "This here's a public right of way. So there's no call to suspicion the motives of others using it, as long as they don't go to ducking for no reason. But let's cross over to the other bank anyways. I like to make folk following me work at it."

The mule didn't argue as they splashed across the shallow desert stream. Longarm rode into a clump of scrub willow and reined in again, hopefully hard to make out in the inky shade of the shimmering willow blades as he stared for a time at the open sand flats and sun-flashed running water of the Santa Cruz. Nobody could have crossed over to his side without him noticing, and nobody had by the time he'd smoked his cheroot down and tossed the butt in the river, saying, "I'm likely just proddy from all that fool talk about Laredo. Even if he's gunning for us, how the hell would he know where to find us right now? We left town by way of Mex Town, from a *posada* no Anglo should know about, right?"

They rode on, stopping now and again to study their back trail, and in less than an hour they were across the Santa Cruz from the Double B spread. So they forded over, studying the layout as they rode in. It was a horse-breeding operation, sure enough. There wasn't enough grass, even close to the river, for cows. He saw they had about forty acres fenced in, with about two dozen ponies trying to share the shade of a clump of cottonwood and more scrub willow. Such grass as they might have originally had fenced in with them was now reduced to scattered patches of what looked more like worn-out shaving brushes. But the thing about raising horses was that you had to feed them oats anyway, so the grazing didn't matter all that much. The ranch house and outbuildings were all low-slung, with adobe walls and sheet-metal roofing. Cunningham had said the outfit hadn't been here long. It hardly took more than one Arizona summer to convince anyone of the advantages of thick Spanish tile.

A dog commenced to bark as Longarm rode up the bank toward the main house. A gal in a calico dress came out, shushed the watchdog, and regarded Longarm thoughtfully with a ten-gauge scattergun cradled casually in the bend of her bare àrm. He reined in and dismounted to lead the mule the rest of the way into shotgun range, raising his empty free hand politely as he called out, "Howdy, ma'am. I'm law, and I'm looking for the Double B."

She called back, "This is the Double B. But my brother's

not here right now. So I'm sorry, but I can't coffee and cake you. Bucky says I'm not to allow strangers in when he's not here."

He moved closer before he said, "You should never tell a stranger you're a woman alone, ma'am. It's best to say your menfolk are out hunting a stray and may be back any minute. I'm reaching in my pocket, now, to show you my badge. You can see my guns is either in my saddle boot or hanging on my other hip. So don't shoot me just yet."

He got out his wallet and flopped it open to let her see his silver federal shield as he held it high between them. She nodded grudgingly. "All right, you can come as far as the shade of the porch."

He tethered the mule to a porch post and saw, now that he could see her better, that she was a young gal of sixteen or so, despite what the wind and summer sun had done to her tired face and straw-colored pigtails. The thin dress was worn out and fit her like a hand-me-down. Her figure under it was a mite thin, too. There was nothing like living on a hardscrabble spread to muscle a gal thin as a teen-age boy. He asked her if her brother's name was really Bucky and when she allowed it was he said, "You'd best hand me that shotgun and sit down, ma'am, for I fear I'm the bearer of news that figures to jar you some."

She did neither, but stared up at him soberly to ask, in an already worn-out voice, "What did you arrest him for this time, Sheriff?"

Longarm said, "I ain't a sheriff. I'm a deputy U.S. marshal and I fear your brother hasn't been arrested. But, since we're on the subject, would you mind telling me how come you thought he might have been, Miss, ah . . . ?"

"Oh, I'm Willy May Bronson. We just came from California to take up this spread Bucky won in a poker game in the Pueblo De Los Angeles. You likely know about the trouble he got into out there, right?"

"Not hardly, ma'am. I'm still waiting for you to tell me about it."

She sighed. "Bucky's never been really vicious. Just a little ambitious for a boy orphaned young and never educated much. He's stolen a few times and gambled a lot more. But he promised me he'd gone straight when we had this chance to make something of ourselves."

Longarm stared thoughtfully around and observed, "I reckon it's possible to make a living, just, raising horses close to town in a horse-killing climate. I sure wish you'd hand me that shotgun and sit down, Miss Willy May."

"What's happened to my brother, if he's not in trouble with the law?" she demanded. "I've been worried sick out here, waiting for him to get back from town. He never said anything about staying in Tucson overnight."

Longarm couldn't think of any way to put it that wouldn't hurt her, so he took the bull by the horns and said, "He had to stay in town, ma'am. He got himself killed there, about this time yesterday afternoon."

Her face went pale, but she didn't faint or even sway as she stared soberly up at him, licked her dry lips, and said, "I knew those men were no good the moment I laid eyes on them! Which one of them murdered my poor brother?"

"Don't know. Who are we talking about, Miss Willy May?"

"There were two of them. A tall man a little younger than you and a shorter, stockier gent mayhaps a mite older. They'd bought horses off us earlier, or, rather, they swapped jaded mounts with Bucky with a little cash to sweeten the deal. Yesterday morning they rode in to ask my brother to go into town with them again, and—"

"Hold it," he cut in. "Did your brother ever leave this spread with 'em on other occasions? It's important, ma'am."

"I'm not sure. They never discussed business in front of

60

me. Not even the time Bucky said they'd given him that money for fresh mounts. He seemed to know them well. I can't tell you why he rode to town with them. Where is my brother's . . . ah . . . ?"

"He's in good hands at the moment, ma'am. Nobody aims to dispose of his mortal remains any way but the way you want it done. I know you want to get right into town to see about it, Miss Willy May. I'm trying not to be brutal. But there's no hurry about your brother's funeral, and I'm sure you'd like to see his killer brought to justice. So we got to talk about them rascals he rode into town with some more."

She sighed and said, "One rode a mare and the other a gelding, both chestnuts. The taller one favored a center-fire saddle and the other roped tie-down. Neither pony was branded."

Longarm nodded soberly. "Lots of folk ride chestnut ponies, Miss Willy May. I'd sure like a more considered notion of what I might see should I ever meet either *dismounted*."

She shrugged. "Neither of 'em looked all that freakful. They were both smooth-shaved, not far from either side of thirty, dressed for serious riding in faded denim outfits with . . . oh, yes, red calico print bandannas and identical gray Stetsons, creased army style. The younger one looked like any innocent cowhand. But, though they both talked polite and respectful to ladies, there was something about the older one as set my teeth on edge. I told my brother there was something sneaky and spiteful about him. But Bucky said they were all right. And now, God damn them both, they've gone and kilt my poor brother!"

Longarm took the shotgun from her gently. "We don't know that, ma'am. As of the moment the men he rode off with, still alive, are just plain suspects. Do you have a

61

picture of your brother handy?"

She nodded. "Sure, how come? You already know what *he* looks like, don't you?"

Longarm said, "When I was younger and greener at this job I thought nothing was certain but death and taxes. Since then I've discovered you don't have to pay taxes if you're rich enough and that folk have been known to I.D. bodies wrong. So before I look any further for your brother's killer, I'd sort of like to make sure it was *him* they killed!"

She looked hopeful as she led him inside. It was darker in her parlor but not much cooler, thanks to the dumb tin roof. He leaned the shotgun against a 'dobe wall and followed her to the unlit fireplace. Its mantel consisted of a railroad tie. He wondered if the Southern Pacific knew. But lots of nesters helped themselves to railroad ties, and it wasn't a federal matter, so he didn't comment. She took a framed tintype from the casually acquired mantel and handed it to him, asking, hopefully, if that was who they were talking about.

The tintype had been taken a spell back, but he had no trouble recognizing the young blonde gal and slightly older boy. The late Bucky Bronson had looked like he suffered from delusions of intelligence even at the age of fourteen or so. The smile on the corpse he'd admired last night hadn't seemed so smug, but it was the same face, damn it.

He removed his hat as he handed the tintype back and said, "I'm sorry, ma'am. But I fear your brother's dead, official, now."

She put the tintype back on the mantel with no change of expression. Then he saw what was about to happen, dropped his hat, and grabbed her as she fainted.

He carried her across the room to a horsehair sofa and laid her gently lengthwise on it with her feet up on one padded arm. Then he went exploring, found a washbasin filled with tepid water in what had to be her bedroom, and soaked his pocket kerchief in it before rejoining her in the parlor. He knelt beside the sofa and sponged her face. Then he unbuttoned her bodice as far down as modesty permitted and spread the wet cloth on her flushed chest. She fluttered her lashes and murmured, sort of confused, "What happened? Where am I, and how did I get here?"

"Lie still and let your brain soak up some more blood, Miss Willy May," he said. "I should be switched for talking so brutal to a lady already on the edge of heatstroke. Do you have any neighbors handy? You're in no shape to ride and I can't see leaving you in this condition. But I can't see staying all that long, neither."

She tried to sit up, saying, "I have to go to town! There's so much to do! I have to see about a proper funeral for Bucky, and with him gone I'll have to see our lawyer, too! Oh, Lord, what's to become of me, with no man to run this spread? I don't know anything about horse breeding! Bucky never let me watch!"

Longarm gently pushed her back down, saying, "Easy, little gal. Let's eat the apple a bite at a time. I already promised you nobody aims to trifle with your brother's remains, and it's too damn hot for a funeral right now in any case. As to your lawyer, I'll send him out if you'll give me his name before I go. He has to be in better shape than you for desert travel, and nothing has to be done right away in any case. I see your stock has shade and a water trough out back, so I'll pump it to the brim and rustle up a bag of feed before I go. As to less delicate details of horse breeding, it's too infernally hot for your stud to worry about, so *you* don't have to, either. Now let's get back to neighbors. I'd like to leave you in she-male hands for a spell."

She blinked her eyes to clear her head. "There's nobody within two miles, save for some trash Injuns camped up the river a ways. Bucky said it was all right, as they was harmless diggers. How come my bodice is so open? Have you

63

been peeping at my . . . you know?"

He shook his head and assured her, "I put a damp cloth atop your fluttersome heart just now, lest it flutter to a halt. But I hardly ever take advantage of unconscious she-males. I want you to keep that in mind, for now I mean to put you properly to bed."

She protested weakly as he scooped her up and carried her into her bedroom. She said, "Put me down!" So he did, on her brass bedstead. Then he pulled off her shoes and stockings and left her calico alone as he fluffed her a pillow, got her under a sheet, and wet the kerchief again to place it, wrung out and folded, on her forehead. He said, "You just stay put till I returns with more delicate help. I don't want you trying to stand till after sundown at the earliest."

"I can't lay slugabed with so many things to worry about!" she protested.

"Sure you can. A maiden in distress has to be a good sport and let folk *help* her, damn it! I said I'd see to your stock. The undertaker in town won't let nothing worse happen to your brother, and you say you have a lawyer to take care of such legal matters as these dismal occasions call for. By the way, are you flat busted? I can stake you to a few bucks if you ain't got even egg money."

She shook her head and said, sort of proudly, "I have almost twenty dollars put away in the coffee can, and my credit in town should be good at least until I can see about selling out. I can't see trying to run the place alone, now. But if our lawyer can get me enough to get back to California with a modest stake, I'll be ever so glad to say goodbye to this infernal heat!"

He told her to hold the thought until he got back directly and left her dreaming about the cool ocean breezes of her happier childhood as he went back out, forked the mule, and rode up the Santa Cruz after Indians.

He spotted the faint blue haze of smoldering wood above

a grove of willows across the streambed. He rode over and found a small band or large family of Papago camped between the riverside and the embankment of the railroad spur to Nogales, where it got close to the river as it more or less followed the route of the more winding Santa Cruz. The Indians had posted a young boy up on the tracks as a lookout. So as Longarm rode in the four grown men of the band were standing with rifles cradled politely across their cotton shirts as they waited to see what happened next.

Longarm dismounted at pistol range and led the mule the rest of the way in, holding his gun hand up in the peace sign. Behind the line of desperately casual men, women and kids peered nervously out from the brush shelters deeper in the willows. Longarm assumed the oldest-looking Papago was the natural leader. He said, "I am sorry I don't speak your nation's language. I am a man in need of help."

The Papago leader stared soberly in silence for a time before he said, "We are not evil people. We have never fought you *Americanos*. Our favorite enemies are the Apache. Our next favorite enemies are the Mexicans, who would have us give up our old gods. Ask the people who moved west in wagons during the great hunt for yellow iron. They will tell you they had trouble with the Apache. They will tell you they had trouble with the Mojave, further west. They will tell you not one white eyes was ever killed by a Papago unless he deserved it. We value the honor of our women as much as any real men do."

Longarm tethered the mule to a willow branch and stood politely, waiting for an invite to move closer. "The Great White Father knows the Papago are good people and values their friendship," he said. "I ride for the Great White Father to enforce his laws. I have never had to arrest a Papago, because everyone knows they are good people."

The older Indian almost smiled as he said, "We know all that. Tell us what you want of us."

Longarm explained about the killing of the nearby horse breeder and the fix his kid sister was in. The old Papago nodded and said, "We will see no evil people raid her until she can find a man to protect her. Her brother was a good person. When we asked his permission to camp here, he did not charge us anything. He did not come over at night with a bottle and try to take advantage of our daughters. If anyone bothers his sister, we will kill them. Is that all you wanted from us?"

Longarm shook his head and said, "The white girl is sick in bed. I think she may have heatstroke on top of the news of her brother's murder. I think it would be a good thing for some of your women to stay in the house with her. I think it would help if you camped on her spread and looked after her stock, at least until her lawyer can help her decide what she should do next. By now others may know her livestock, land, and water are not too well defended. If it is true you found them good neighbors, I ask you to help."

"You *trust* us, white eyes? Have you not heard thieving Indians can't be trusted inside a fence, or that we always rape white-eyed women we find alone and unprotected?"

"One hears a lot of things about lots of people. If I did not think Papago were good people, I would not have come to you."

For the first time the old man smiled. Then he said, "Ride back ahead of us to tell my white-eyed daughter we are on our way. It will only take us a few minutes to break camp."

Chapter 5

A couple of hours later the sun had moved some across the cobalt-blue bowl of the Arizona sky, but it glared down just as balefully as Longarm rode toward Tucson. He and the mule were cutting directly across the cactus flats, now that they had the way figured better. But, though he knew the shorter way to town, he didn't know much more about other matters than the tedious ride had justified. He'd helped the dead boy's sister as much as anyone could help at such dismal times, and once he met up with her lawyer he might be able to help a mite more. For in truth the teen-aged Willy May had as much business running an Arizona spread alone as he had operating on somebody's brain in the dark. He'd gotten to know the layout better, helping the Indians set up before he left, and how in thunder the late Bucky Bronson had meant to show a steady income out of such a shoestring operation eluded Longarm entirely.

He had something else bothering him as the higher parts of Tucson kept retreating from him like a mirage above the cactus pads ahead. The hairs on the back of his neck kept informing Longarm that he had company on his back trail. But every time he looked back, there was nothing to be seen in the shimmering view but bone-white desert and a variety of tedious cactus species. He told the mule, "Well, if nobody pegs a shot at us in the near future, we'll soon have you back in your shady stall. But don't keep trying to grab the bit like that, damn it. I'll let you run the last mile home. But I aim to return you alive, not lathered to death."

The mule paid him little heed and kept trying to burst into a trot as even Longarm could see they were getting closer to town at last. He aimed for a gap in a solid wall of prickly pear ahead and, when the mule tried to bolt, reined him back to a dancing walk and swore at him. Then Longarm had a better notion, grinned, and said, "All right, mule. Powder River and let her buck! *Run,* you dumb jackass, and see if I care!"

The mule obliged by dashing through the cactus gap at a dead run. As they passed through, Longarm drew his saddle gun and rolled out of the saddle, landing on his feet and running some, himself, to keep from falling before he could lever a round in the chamber of his Winchester.

Then, as the mule scampered happily out of sight for home, Longarm turned to cover the gap in the cactus and, sure enough, heard approaching hoofbeats as whoever had been ghosting him spurred his own mount to keep from losing him entirely. So Longarm had the drop on him as he tore through the same gap, not looking right or left, which was an awful mistake on his part. Longarm snapped, "All right, Laredo!"

Then he saw it wasn't Laredo, but some son of a bitch he'd never seen before. But since said son of a bitch was swinging the muzzle of a Remington his way as he reined in, Longarm fired first and blew him off his chestnut mare.

The downed rider's mount ran on. Mounts were like that, when thirsty as well as spooked by gunfire. So Longarm walked thoughtfully over through the settling dust, recocking his Winchester, to see how he'd made out with that first round.

He'd aimed pretty well, considering. The stranger lay face down with his hands sort of groping for the gray Stetson and Remington saddle gun in the dust way ahead of him. A puddle of blood nestled in the fold of his blue denim jacket between his shoulder blades. Longarm had shot him from the other side. Forty-four-forty slugs were like that at close range. Longarm knelt to feel the side of his throat, anyway, before he said, "Yep. You're dead. Let's see who the hell you was."

He rolled the limp body on its bloody back. The dusty face was strange to him. It had a moustache bigger than Longarm's, so that let off the two Willy May had described to him. But Billy Vail had said there were at least a dozen in the gang. Longarm told the dead man, "Let's see if I got this right, pard. The two who rode into town with Bronson are likely long gone. You was left to keep an eye on the trail to the Double B, to see how long it took someone to put two and two together. Yeah, that works. You never followed me from town. You was laying for me, waiting for a chance to backshoot me. We'd best put that on the back of the stove for now. You had plenty of chances out there for a long shot, even if you was yellow. Let's see what your pockets has to say about you."

They didn't have much. The dead man had smoked Bull Durham and cheated at cards, judging from the way the poker deck in a breast pocket was marked. He had over fifty dollars in his wallet, but no I.D. Since the money was of little use in tracing anyone back to anywhere, Longarm put it in his own wallet, lest it just go to waste. He left the small change in the pants pocket alone. It was best to leave *some* money in the official report he'd have to hand in sooner or later.

Longarm already had a pocketknife and no use at all for either a single-action sidearm or another saddle gun. The pocketwatch he found was cheaper than his own. He eyed the fancy spurs strapped to the dead rider's Justins with more interest. Everything else about the gent was sort of nondescript, but big sunburst rowels of the spurs pointed at a rider given to cruelty to animals or sudden desires for speed. Nobody this side of the border inlaid gunmetal-blue steel with coin silver leaves and flowers so skillfully. Longarm nodded and told the dead man, "You bought or stole them spurs in Old Mexico, or mighty close, old son. Nobody but a dude or a Southwesterner would be caught dead in such fancy spurs but, come to think of it, you *have*."

Longarm rose, dusted off his knee, and said, "Well, you just stay put and I'll send someone out for you with a buckboard." Then he rolled the body back on its face lest a buzzard find it before it could be picked up and photographed for future reference.

Longarm started trudging his way toward Tucson, sincerely hoping he'd been right about it not being more than a mile or so to the city limits. Long before he got there he spotted Mexican sombreros as well as dust above the cactus ahead, and he holed up in some prickly pear until he saw it was El Gato and some of his riders.

As Longarm stepped into view, the young Mexican outlaw reined in and asked, "What happened? Your mule came in without you, *amigo!*"

"I was hoping it would. McClellan saddles is expensive. I just shot it out with another Anglo about half a mile out. Guess who won?"

El Gato grinned. "I'll ride you," he said. So Longarm handed his saddle gun to another Mexican, took El Gato's helping hand, and forked across the saddle skirts behind El Gato, who naturally asked which way they were going now.

Longarm said, "Back to town. I'll send someone from

70

the coroner out to gather the remains, and I has to see a lawyer before closing time."

El Gato said that was jake with him and as they rode back to town together Longarm politely brought the rebel and his pals more or less up to date, save for the unguarded horses out at the Double B. There was no sense in tempting wayward youths past reason.

El Gato opined that all the indications pointed to the main body of the gang being south, either in the border town of Nogales or across the border entirely. He said, "The one who tried to bushwhack you just now sounds like a rear guard to me."

Longarm said, "Maybe. But why leave a rear guard so *far* behind you? Nogales is over sixty miles south, a good four days' ride in this infernal climate."

"Faster by train, no?"

"I wasn't riding a train. I was riding a mule, and the only train south for days left some time go. It looks more to me like the gent I just met up with is *setting* on something."

"But on what, *amigo?* Treasure buried somewhere along the trail south?"

"It only works part way. My office tells me some of them stolen bonds was just cashed in Mexico. Deep. Tell me something, El Gato. If I was to ride due south and jump the border say near Nogales, how would I go about swinging over to Chihuahua without getting in lots of trouble? The last time I tried crossing the Sierra Madres peaceable I run into everything from *you* to Rurales and Yaqui Indians almost as mean."

El Gato shrugged and replied, "If it was not possible, my *muchachos* and me would not be this far west, of course. But we have much hair on our chests and, in a pinch, we can pass for simple *vaqueros*. A gringo gang could *fight* their way from Nogales to Chihuahua, if they were tough

71

enough. But not without leaving traces of their long passage in the form of shot-up Mexican lawmen and lawless Indians. In all modesty, I must confess my own recent activities in the cause of liberty have stirred up a *muy grande* hornet's nest in northwest Mexico of late."

Longarm chuckled dryly and said, "I read the papers. I hope you won't take this personal, El Gato, but I also know for a fact that old Captain Morales, in command of los Federales just south of Nogales, is one of the few such officers as can't be bought."

El Gato frowned. "Morales? I piss on his mother's grave and shit in his sister's face, because she is too ugly for anyone but Morales to fuck! He is a dedicated sucker of cocks and killer of women and children! He is, in other words, a typical Federale!"

Longarm said, "Don't get your bowels in an uproar, old son. I never said Captain Morales was *nice*. I just said he can't be bought, and he hates us *Americanos* to the point of dispolite. So I can't see him easing the passage of any gringo gang through his well-patrolled territory, and it's an established fact the Yaqui one meets in the *less* well-patrolled parts of the Sierra Madre want to fight everyone, *Mexican, Americano,* or just plain stranger of any complexion or political persuasion, right?"

El Gato shrugged and answered, "*Si,* everyone knows Yaqui are simply insane. Even Apache avoid them. Nonetheless, if someone cashed those bonds in Chihuahua, someone got through. Unless we hear, soon, about a lot of noise south of the border, someone got through most *sneaky,* too! What are you going to do, sneak into Mexico yourself, again?"

Longarm sighed. "My boss told me not to. Last time I come close to starting another Mexican War, for some reason. On the other hand, I still got orders to round up them bank robbers and, if I can't find 'em on this side of the border, I may have to bend the rules some, again. Old Billy hardly ever fires me for disobeying orders if I *win*. When an Anglo lawman *loses,* down Mexico way, he's seldom in any condition to be fired, in any case."

Lawyer Frankenberg turned out to be a pleasant surprise, since Longarm had expected her to be a German band or at least a *him*. But when he got to her office a block from the depot he found Lawyer Frankenberg was a gal about thirty and a mighty handsome honey blonde despite her black poplin dress and the granny glasses perched on her perky little nose. The bodice of her severe dress was filled out nicely, too.

She led him into her pine-paneled office and offered him a bentwood chair as she sat behind a desk as big but not as well made as Billy Vail's. He scored one point with her right off by not asking what in thunder a she-male was doing with a law degree. He knew lots of gals had come out West to be lawyers, doctors, and such in less stuffy surroundings. When a territorial town elected drunks to the city council and hung badges on ex-convicts, it likely didn't matter as much.

She said it was jake with her if he smoked, so he lit up and proceeded to bring her up-to-date about the troubles of the Bronson kids. When he'd finished, she brushed a strand of hair from her forehead and said, "Oh, Lord, that tears it for poor little Willy May, then. I tried more than once to get her brother to make out a will. I only charge five dollars for the paperwork. But he was one of those happy-go-lucky types who think they're immortal. So he died *intestate* and Willy May, damn it, is a *minor* as well as a mere female!"

Longarm said, "I noticed. Where does that leave her, ma'am? She says she'd like to sell out and go back to California. Ain't that possible?"

The lady lawyer shrugged. "It's possible. It's just going

to take a lot of work on my part. Her brother's estate, such as it is, will have to go through probate. The judge will surely award the estate to her, since I know of no other heirs. But it's going to take *time*, and, when *that's* cleared up, she'll still be an underaged mere female with no powers to dispose of or even manage her own property. They're going to insist on a court-appointed guardian."

Longarm took a thoughtful drag on his cheroot and asked, "Can't that be you, ma'am? No offense, but you don't look underage. You must be about twenty-one or two, right?"

She smiled wanly. "Thank you, sir. I'm still a mere female."

Longarm frowned and said, "That's the third time you've low-rated my favorite sex as *mere*, ma'am. I've read some of Miss Virginia Woodhull's writings on the short end of the stick some of you ladies seem to feel we menfolk has handed you. But fair is fair, and if the gents here in Tucson don't mind you being an officer of the court, how come you can't manage the affairs of a young client?"

She said, "As a territory, Arizona is under federal law, save for local town ordinances. As a federal officer, you surely know that, while a woman can legally manage property left to her by her husband, unless she marries again, the federal courts frown on any mere female managing the property of *other* people!"

She took off her glasses and pinched herself between her closed eyes before she went on. "Oh, it makes me so mad! You're a man. So you'll never know what it feels like in court when an ignorant frontier lawyer with tobacco juice dribbling down his vest calls you 'little lady' and winks at a cowboy jury as if they all know something dirty about you that you don't know!"

"You may be carrying more of a cross than was issued you," Longarm said. "For I've had many a lawyer wink at the jury behind *my* back, too, and whatever the joke was, they let the skunk I'd arrested off. This unjust world is filled with injustices great and small, Lawyer Frankenberg. You don't have to be she-male, colored, or even Indian to get taken advantage of. It's a fact of life that them in the habit of low-rating others will low-rate them any way they can. I'm white and they let me wear pants. So the same lawyer as called you a silly twittering she-male in court would likely call me an ignorant country boy who don't know the rules of evidence. If I went up against him wearing specs and waving a degree from Harvard he'd be just as willing to dismiss me as an Eastern dude who naturally can't savvy the way the law works out West. So I've found it more comfortsome to just be my plain old self and not worry about it. Some folk like you no matter what you are, while those who don't like you are going to find something spiteful to say about you no matter who you might be. Can we get back to a young gal in *real* trouble, now? If you're her lawyer, it's up to you to get her out of it."

The blonde stared soberly across at him and said, "You do have a way of making your brief short and to the point, don't you? You're right, of course. I'll have to think of something, as soon as I get rid of this headache. It's impossible to think straight in this awful heat. But I'll go over the books after sundown and a cold bath and—"

"I got some questions of my own you won't have to look up," Longarm cut in. As she stared at him with a puzzled smile, Longarm said, "The little gal told me her brother got the spread by winning at cards. I just left the place, and it don't seem to me he won all that much. Desert land sells for a dollar or so an acre and you couldn't give that house free to a smart Mexican. Their livestock is scrub and they're low on fodder. The only thing of real value they have is riparian rights, and—"

"You *know* about riparian law?" she cut in, with renewed interest in his handsome but, in truth, unshaven and trail-dusty features.

Longarm shrugged. "I'm a lawman, so I have to know something about law. As I was saying, their claim includes a stretch of the only river in this part of Arizona that don't run bone-dry by the Fourth of July. They got two pumps saying the water table can't be more'n thirty-odd feet under their land, too. But they only own a bitty stretch of water rights with a mess of mighty empty land as good all around. So, even selling everything from firewood to riparian rights in one tempting package, Miss Willy May ain't never going to wind up rich, and I can't help wondering how they managed to survive at all on such a puny spread."

The lady lawyer said, "Apparently it wasn't easy. Bucky sold scrub ponies now and then, and gambled twice as often. He always seemed to be able to scrape up just enough at tax time, dealing three-card monte in the saloons of an evening."

"Did you ever see him win dime one at cards, ma'am?"

"Good heavens, do I look like I hang out in saloons, even if they'd let me? He told me he was lucky at cards when I asked him, one time, where he'd managed to scrape up some money just in the nick of time."

Longarm said, "I ain't accusing *you* of fibbing, ma'am. I'm accusing the late Bucky Bronson. For when they brought him in dead from the town dump, not a man in town could identify him. They naturally didn't show him to you or any of the other few who might have known him on sight. But don't it strike you odd that a boy who played for money in the saloons, regular, managed to do so with his face unknown to the spit-and-whittle gang who patronize them? Hardly any saloon lets a gent deal three-card monte wearing a mask."

She blinked and said, "My God, you said he cashed a

stolen bearer bond at the main bank in town, too!"

"I did. By the way, did him and his sister have an account you know of at any *other* bank in town?"

She shook her head. "I'm sure they didn't. You're right about Bucky living day-to-day. But if he wasn't selling more stock than I thought, and wasn't gambling for eating money, as he said . . . I can't believe it. I'll confess I never thought much of the poor boy's mental capacity, but I just can't see him as a *crook!*"

Longarm blew a thoughtful smoke ring and explained, "My job would be a whole lot easier if even *half* the crooks looked like crooks to the average person, ma'am. There's a boy running loose in New Mexico right now who looks so innocent folks wonder how come his mama lets him out after dark. His real name's Henry McArthy, but you may have heard of him as Billy the Kid. The body over to the undertaker's at the moment looks twice as tough."

"I still can't see poor Bucky doing anything really vicious," she insisted.

Longarm said, "That's funny. His kid sister says much the same. He was a mite wild, but never vicious. They say old Jesse James is mighty fond of women and children, too, wherever he's hiding out right now, after acting vicious enough for most innocent lads his age."

She heaved a defeated sigh and said, "All right. In just what way do you think Bucky might have been involved in the robbery of the Maricopa bank, Deputy Long?"

"Ain't no 'might' about it. He had to be involved in some way, unless you want to figure the tooth fairy left that stolen bond under his pillow. I wish you'd call me Custis, by the way. Saves spit on such a hot, dry day."

She laughed and told him in that case he could call her Erica, and he said he sure would. When she asked him what he meant by *some* way, Longarm explained, "Since he can't tell us, and I ain't caught anyone who could, yet, I'm keep-

77

ing an open mind on just how deeply he was mixed up in the holdup itself. He had to be at least a receiver of stolen goods, and if anyone in the gang gave him hot bonds for a fresh mount they was *both* fools. I figure he sold horses to at least someone bound for Mexico in a hurry, since his sister told me he did. But Willy May can't put more'n two possible gang members on or about the property at the same time. So, like I said, I'm still trying to figure out more than I know, yet."

"Couldn't they have split up after the robbery, Custis?" Erica asked.

He nodded. "It sure looks that way. I do have a fuzzy pattern sort of emerging from the mists, but, I dunno, have you ever had the funny feeling someone was trying to razzle-dazzle you with numbers that just don't add sensible?"

"You ask a question like that of a *lawyer?*" She smiled. "I don't have much trouble fitting the pieces you have so far together, Custis. If they hadn't split up right after the robbery, someone would have reported a large band of riders on the open desert by now. If they'd all made it to Mexico together, all the stolen bearer bonds would have been cashed, not just one rider's share. So, obviously, some of the gang have to be long gone while others, at least that one you just shot it out with a little while ago, are still in the territory, for some reason. What if part of their loot was left with the Bronson kids for safe keeping and Bucky, needing money in a hurry, cashed a bond against orders?"

"Already been around that barn," Longarm said. "It only works to a point. If some of the gang left loot with Bronson and he double-crossed 'em, that would account for his early demise. But why would they hang around Tucson, *after?* I found Willy May undefended out to the Double B. I don't mean to brag, but it do seem a man willing to go up against *me* with a gun would be brave enough to take on a skinny little gal alone with an old muzzle-loader."

"What if it was buried somewhere on the property rather than in the house?"

"That'd make it even easier, wouldn't it? She has a watch-dog out there. But after it barked at me once it slunk off and never even growled at me again. So after dark a man could dig up anything anywhere on the property. But I don't think there's anything out there to dig. Aside from it making no sense for it to be there, I poked about some, getting the little gal and the Indians forted up right. I'd have noticed if anyone had been digging much in the bone-dry, rock-hard earth around the house. The house itself has solid adobe walls and a dirt floor. So that didn't leave many hidey-holes, and I confess I looked in the few I noticed."

"Without a search warrant?" She dimpled in mock severity.

He grinned back and said, "Didn't need one. I was invited in. I told you I know my law. But let's forget what might or might not have been in the possession of the late Bucky Bronson until recent. He ain't got it now. His sister don't have it neither. So why in thunder was that jasper after me with a Remington this afternoon? To keep me from reporting something I might have discovered out to the Double B? I wasn't even sure the Bronson boy was a crook until you told me he was a liar just now. I think I'm being misdirected, Erica."

"What?" She frowned. But he didn't want to explain magic tricks again to someone who didn't have a gun on her hip. So he just got to his feet and said he'd tell her what he meant when he had a better notion what that might be. She rose, too, and handed him her card, with her home address on it. She asked him to get in touch with her, night or day, as soon as he found anything out. She said it could be important to her client.

She asked him where she'd be able to look him up, if need be, and when he told her politely that he'd rather not say, she smiled wanly and allowed that she understood. So they shook and he went downstairs to open the furnace door again.

He stuck to the shady side of the street as he worked his way back to the hub of town. He got to the bank he'd meant to call on next and saw they were closed for the day. He checked the time with his pocketwatch and cursed himself for not having gone there first, for he'd only missed their three o'clock closing by ten minutes. He pounded on the door, knowing the clerks at least might still be working on the books inside. But a wary-looking old gent packing an old Patterson conversion on his hip and wearing a private bank guard badge came to the far side of the glass to point at the sign and wave Longarm off. Longarm doubted the old coot knew much about cashing bearer bonds, so he went.

His next sensible stop would be the Western Union office. He had little news for the home office, but by now they might have something new to tell him. He clung to the shade as far as he could. Then he bit the bullet and headed over to the sunny side of the street. Thanks to the angle of the afternoon sun, the shadows of the buildings behind him made it almost to the middle of the dusty thoroughfare. So when someone popped over the top of a false front behind him, Longarm spotted his shadow, leaped sideways, and came down facing the frame building, gun in hand, just as the rooftop bushwhacker's first round spanged a mushroom of alkali dust from the place where Longarm would have been if he hadn't changed his mind so sudden.

The unknown ducked down behind the false front as he saw the odds were more even now. Longarm fired through the planking, drilling a neat hole in a hat-store sign and, when he heard a yip of pain, drilling another through the lower curve of the letter S. Then he was running for the storefront as an old lady in a mother hubbard popped out of her door like a cuckoo and yelled at him to stop before she called the law on him. He paid her no mind as he made for the slit between her frame store and the 'dobe building next to it. As he had expected, an outside stairway ran up the side of the flat-topped 'dobe, Spanish style. But when he eased up to the rooftops, there was nobody up there but him. He leaped across to the tarpaper roof of the hat store and moved to the far side to curse when he saw another way down in the form of a ladder. He strode over to the back of the false front. The bright sunlight glinted on spent brass from a .44-40, so he knew how lucky he'd just been. The rascal had tried to gun him with a rifle, not a pistol. Only repeating rifles threw brass.

He couldn't find any blood, so he couldn't tell if he'd winged the son of a bitch or just scared a yip out of him. It had surely sounded like a flesh-wound yip. But if it had been, he hadn't hurt the bastard half as much as he'd aimed to.

Longarm went down the ladder to study the footprints in the dust between the old woman's shop and the next one. There were too many, coming in all shapes and sizes. The narrow shortcut was naturally known, and used, by lots of townees. A she-male voice demanded, "What are you doing in there, you wicked boy?"

He turned, reloading his gun, to explain to the old woman who he was and why he'd been stomping about her roof just now. She was still mighty steamed until he holstered his sidearm, took out his wallet, and gave her a couple of bucks for the sign painter.

As they parted friendlier out front, Marshal Cunningham came charging up the shady side of the street, trailing two deputies Longarm didn't know. He told the town law what had just happened, adding, "It's too damned hot to go through the usual futile motions, boys. The cuss may turn up at some doctor's office if I really hit him. If I didn't, he won't. So let *me* worry about him."

Cunningham said, "We ain't greedy. But you do seem calm for a man who lives such an active life, Longarm. Any notion who it might have been?"

Longarm shrugged and said, "Doubt if it could have been you or me. After that, it gets less clear. Did my Mex pals deliver that one I shot earlier to you, Marshal?"

"They did, and that's another thing I wanted to discuss with you. I know you're law, and they say you hardly ever shoot folks just to be mean, but I ain't used to having corpses delivered by buckboard C.O.D. In the future I'd be obliged if you come in person to tell me who you just shot and why. The greasers as brung that dead cowhand in off the desert spoke tolerable English, but all I could get outten 'em was that you blew the rascal off his horse a mile outside of town and that he didn't have a thing in his pockets when they fetched him in for you."

Longarm sighed. "I might have known. Oh, well, if they left him his boots he's ahead. What they told you was close enough to the little I know about him. He was following me back from the Double B. I meant to ask him why. But as he was waving a Remington at me, I never got the chance. He describes the same way the gents who held up the Maricopa bank did, save for not having a mask and slicker on when I gunned him. We found a yellow slicker in his bedroll, though. His chestnut ran into town and some Mex kids took charge of it lest it starve. Willy May Bronson described me two others as fit. She said they had on red print calico neckerchiefs when they swapped ponies out to the Double B with her late brother."

Cunningham said, "Hot damn! The gang rid outten Maricopa with the same kind of kerchiefs over their faces! Did the gal say which way they went?"

"Yeah, the second time they come by. She said they rode off most anywhere the first time, a few days after the bank robbery. Then they came back from who knows where and asked her brother to ride into town with 'em. That's the last she seen of them, or her brother, alive."

Cunningham frowned. "Something's missing. Tucson ain't quite as big as Kansas City, you know. The Bronson kid was barely known in town. So that makes three strangers riding in by broad day, and not a soul in town saw fit to mention it to me or my boys?"

"Try her this way," Longarm said. "They circled. The two mysterious riders rode around to the city dump. Then they put young Bronson on the ground with the rest of the trash and rode off, leading his pony."

"That works, but *why?*"

"Wouldn't have been polite to gun him in front of his kid sister. Or they wanted him found sooner with that crispy five-dollar bill on him. I think they got him to cash one of the bonds for them. He may have done other dishonest things in the past, judging from the way he said he gambled when nobody recalls gambling with him, and . . . Damn, that's it! The one I just gunned was carrying a poker deck he should have been ashamed of. They may not even have had to lead the poor kid down the primrose path. They may have slickered him into *owing* 'em, and got him to cash that bond as a way to pay 'em back. Then, having used him as a tool to cover their own tracks, they gunned him lest he ever be used as a witness by *us!*"

Cunningham nodded grimly and said, "I'm glad nobody actually residing in Tucson township ties in with that gang direct. But they sure used the boy shameful for a lousy few dollars. A white man who'd kill another for less'n a hundred dollars would eat shit. But it happens more often than it should. I'd best see about sending someone out to comfort his poor sis."

Longarm explained about the friendly Indians and the

83

lady lawyer looking after Willy May, and Cunningham looked relieved. He headed back to his office as Longarm went on across to the Western Union.

A wire from Denver was waiting for him there. Billy Vail said the Texas Rangers had arrested a Mexican businessman in Del Rio when he tried to cash one of the hot bonds at a bank there. But they'd had to let him go when he was able to prove he'd bought them at a discount from a Mexican banker in Durango. The Treasury Department had sent a wire to said Mexican bank, but so far nobody down that way had seen fit to reply, and it didn't seem likely they meant to. Some Mexicans still seemed mad about the misunderstandings of 1848, for some reason.

Vail ended his wire with an order to Longarm to return to Denver and stop sniffing at cold trails. Longarm didn't send back the night letter he'd meant to. There was nothing cold about Arizona at the moment, and if he hadn't picked up the direct order yet he could hardly be fussed at for disregarding it.

He got out his notebook and consulted it to see what he ought to do next. It was too hot as well as too early for supper, and saloons smelled awful this time of the afternoon. He decided he still had time to check out the big-shot banker Laredo was said to work for. It would be interesting to see how Laredo was feeling about now.

He'd left his mount in the Mexican quarter, so he walked to the banker's address in the more fashionable part of town. It was naturally far, so he regretted not having the mule under him by the time he got to the place.

The house was whitewashed adobe with its front veranda shaded by cottonwoods. He knew cottonwood could grow on less water than some trees, but the banker sure had money to spend like water indeed, if he had any sort of trees at all in his Tucson dooryard. When Longarm knocked, a Mexican gal came to the door to say the master wasn't home and the mistress wasn't receiving guests. Longarm said, "That's all right. I ain't a guest, I'm the law." So the maid said she'd see what the lady had to say about that.

She came back in a few minutes and told Longarm to follow her. She led him to a back room where a sultry brunette reclined on a red velvet sofa, dressed for the climate in a Spanish lace dressing gown. He could see she wore nothing under it, which was sensible but sort of shocking, with the lace woven so openwork.

The banker's wife, if that was who she was, knew better than to rise in an outfit like that. She had her shapely legs crossed as she smiled up at him innocently, considering, and said, "Forgive my dress. I never have gotten used to the summers here. That will be all, Maria."

The maid left them alone as the brunette on the sofa waved Longarm to a seat at the foot of it, said she was Lila Mansfield, and that it was all right if he smoked. That made her the banker's wife, all right. He wondered if she knew he could see her nipples through that lace. He wondered if she cared. It wasn't his problem, so he put his hat aside and lit a cheroot as she studied him like a spoiled, lazy house cat. He told her who he was and that he already knew her husband's bank wasn't the one that had cashed the stolen bond. Then he said, "What I'm most interested in is your husband's hired bodyguard, Laredo. Would he be anywheres about, ma'am?"

Lila made a wry face. "Hardly. By now he and my husband are in Maricopa. Wilson left for there on the noonday train. He left with quite a bit of money, so naturally he took his tame ape with him. What's Laredo gotten himself into this time with the law?"

Longarm smiled. "Nothing, if he wasn't in town just now. Could I ask how come your husband left for Maricopa with a mess of money, ma'am?"

She hesitated, then shrugged and said, "Why not? You heard about the bank robbery they had in Maricopa, didn't you?"

"Something about it, ma'am. Not too many details."

"Well, naturally there was a run on the bank when people heard it was missing so much money. They have to cover the government bonds left in their vaults for safekeeping, too. So they wired my husband for help and he's lending them a hundred thousand, at six percent, of course."

Longarm didn't comment. He'd never met a banker yet who lent money free. If Laredo had an alibi and banker Mansfield was lending money to the bank in Maricopa instead of sticking it up, he'd just run out of sensible things to ask a lady in a scandalous outfit. So he was about to excuse himself when, outside, all hell busted loose.

Lila Mansfield leaped to her feet with a cry of delight as lightning flashed again and it commenced to rain fire and salt outside from what had been a clear blue desert sky just a minute or so ago. Desert skies were like that. The shapely, almost naked gal ran to a sash window and swung it open, gasping, "Oh, God, doesn't that feel glorious!" Raindrops big enough for minnows to live in bounced off the sill and spattered her all down the front of her thin lace. As she turned around he could see that she was either wearing a mighty small French G-string or was hairy as hell between the legs. It was hard to tell as she sat back down, crossed her damned thighs again, and said, with an odd little smile, "I fear you're marooned with me until the dove gets back with that olive branch."

He nodded and said, "It sure is a gullywasher. But it'll likely be over soon, lest the saguaros burst their green skins. These desert showers never last long enough to really matter. But I'd say we're in for a cooler afternoon than usual. Might even be a one-blanket night. Hope no greenhorns is camped in a dry wash right now."

He'd meant to cheer her with his observations on the local climate, but for some reason she was scowling thoughtfully. He asked her why and she said, "I was hoping it would stay hot. I know full well my husband means to miss the night train with considerable ingenuity and spend the night with that infernal Peggy Gordon. But I was hoping they'd be too hot and sweaty to enjoy themselves."

Longarm frowned and said, "Only Peggy Gordon I ever heard of was a mean-hearted woman in an old Scotch song, Miss Lila."

She nodded. "It's not her real name. Whores never use their real names. And the Peggy Gordon in Maricopa is more than mean-hearted. She's a damned bitch! Wilson told me when we married up that he'd given up visiting such women, but you men are all alike."

He wondered how she knew so much about men playing slap and tickle with women of low repute. It wouldn't have been polite to ask, so he never. He'd learned that sometimes folk told a lawman more than they might have meant to if he just kept still and gave them the chance. So he leaned back, enjoying his cheroot as the room kept cooling off and the sultry gal at the far end of the sofa seemed to be steaming up. He wondered if the banker she was married up with knew he might have Laredo guarding the wrong body. He wondered less as Lila said, "That bitch is older and fatter than I am! What makes you men so blind? Can't you see that under all that paint and henna rinse she's just a cheap old bawd?"

Longarm smiled. "I've never seen Miss Peggy Gordon in my life, Miss Lila," he said. She sneered. "She's hardly a *Miss*, damn it. She's a *Madam* Gordon, if you know what I mean," she said scornfully.

"Sort of. I never go to such places myself, save on duty. I'm too romantic-natured."

She laughed like a mean little kid. "I can see you'd seldom have to pay for *your* loving. Are those shoulders real, or have they started padding shirts as well this season? Why don't you take off your shirt and vest, at least, and get comfortable? It's not that cool yet, and you can see you're among friends."

He started to say he felt just fine the way he was. Not because he wanted her to think him a sissy, but because it was dumb to undress with a married gal right in her husband's study. On the other hand, sometimes a lawman had to sacrifice his principles while questioning suspects and, if she wasn't out to seduce him for some suspicious reason, she was just naturally horny as hell as well as built mighty nice.

He stood up, took off his gun rig, and hung it over a nearby chair. Then he stripped to the waist. She gasped, "My God, you have a lovely body! This is one time revenge will be a *pleasure!*"

He'd figured that might be what she had in mind. He moved over to the door and locked it as, behind him, Lila said, "Pooh, my servants are trained never to come unless I ring for them." So he moved back to the sofa, sat on the edge, and proceeded to remove his boots and pants as she giggled and slipped out of her lace. "I admire a man who gets right down to business," she said.

Then she saw what he had to offer as he turned her way to take her in his arms and gasped, "My God, is all that meant for me!"

But once he'd mounted her, sure enough she was so love-gushed it went in with hardly any effort at all, even though she said he was killing her. He kissed her hard to shut her up as he began to move his hard-on inside her. She moved back, bumping and grinding like he'd figured she might have learned before her husband made an honest woman of her. He'd wondered if her bitterness about her husband doing this with another gal about now could be professional jealousy.

Great minds must have been running in the same channel. For as they came together fast and came up for air, Lila laughed and said, "I'll bet Wilson and that cheap Peggy Gordon are taking advantage of this same rain the same way. But, you know what? She's not getting laid as good as *I* am! My God, you've got such a beautiful tool, and you use it so nicely, too!"

He knew he was expected to say her husband couldn't be getting as nice a lay no matter what the other gal looked like, but he found it distasteful to discuss other men at times like these. He'd never figured out why so many women seemed to want to. Lila was pretty, she kissed just swell, and she screwed as good as it was possible. But he was already starting to wish he hadn't been so weak-willed. He said, "Look, I'm on top of you right now because I likes to be there. If all you're getting out of this is a chance to mean-mouth others, I'd best just finish and be on my way, hear?"

Suiting deeds to his words, Longarm got an elbow under each of Lila's knees and hauled her thighs up and open as far as they could spread as he rammed her hard and fast to get it over with. She gasped, "Not so hard! Not so deep! You're hurting me, and . . . Oh, my God, I think I'm really going to. . . . No, I know I am! I'm *commmming!*"

He'd thought that was the general idea, but he'd suspected she'd faked her first orgasm with him. He suspected she did, a lot, when she was out for so-called revenge on her wayward husband. Women sure were sneaky about such matters.

Then he stopped wondering why and just let himself go in her as she moaned and groaned she was coming again and that if he didn't run off to California with her and all her husband's money she'd kill herself or something. He lay limp atop her, getting his breath back, as the rain pounded on the roof above. He chuckled and when she asked what was so funny he said, "I'll never understand you gals, as much fun as it is to try. You never seem to think about nothing but men. You powder and paint yourselves up to tempt us poor brutes as much as you can, and then when you manage to lead a man astray with all your she-male witchcraft, you can't make up your minds if you like it or not."

"We have more delicate feelings," she pouted.

He said, "I'll buy that. But why do you go to so much infernal trouble making menfolk want you if you ain't sure you want *them?* When a man wants sex, he's likely to screw a knothole if it don't watch out. But when he ain't in the mood, he don't even take a bath."

She laughed and said, "You smell clean, for Arizona. But then you're *always* in the mood, aren't you?"

"Likely more often than I ought to be."

"Good. Would you please screw my knothole some more? For some reason, I don't give a damn what my husband's doing right now. Peggy Gordon's welcome to him, now that I've found someone that more than fills his shoes."

It wasn't exactly the banker's shoes he was filling at the moment. But after he'd made her come a few more times in more interesting positions, they were such good pals she even invited him to supper. He said he was much obliged, but he had a train to catch. She asked to where, and if she could come with him. He told her he aimed to hop a freight to Nogales and that girls wasn't allowed in the caboose. It was a lie, but a white lie, for it just wouldn't have been proper to carry the banker's wife to Maricopa with him on any kind of train. He'd once been caught in the crossfire between two jealous she-males, and it had been noisy as hell.

Chapter 6

Longarm didn't tell anyone else in Tucson he was catching the suppertime SP to Maricopa. He already had the timetable in his pocket, and it might be interesting to see who might or might not be waiting for him at the far end. The Pullman stopping at Tucson was a through train from the East and wasn't meant to stop at bitty towns like Maricopa. But when he showed the conductor his badge and bet him a dollar the train couldn't even slow down at Maricopa, the conductor said he'd already lost. So Longarm found a seat in the club car and sipped beer for a spell as he watched the scenery on the way.

The tracks ran in line with the Santa Cruz a spell, and he'd been right about that unexpected rain doing wonders for the river's health. The rain had let up even before he'd left Lila on her sofa with a wistful, dreamy smile on her pretty face. But the runoff from the washes all about had turned the shallow braided Santa Cruz into a fair imitation of the Mississippi and saguaros stood waist-deep in water a quarter of a mile from the regular banks, looking surprised as hell. The main channel was churning muddy water like a steamboat wake, with driftwood, dead cows, beer bottles, and such bobbing north lickety-split. The trouble with the Santa Cruz, as rivers went, was that you couldn't navigate it at low water or high, and it never seemed to be anything else. That left two ways for people to move up and down the Santa Cruz, leaving out plain walking as just plain loco. You could ride a mount or you could mount a train. He didn't question anyone on this one about suspicious passengers. He knew everyone else working for the law in these parts already had, and he'd read what the train crews had to say about the notion. It was possible for one or two gents traveling sedate to board the train most anywhere, though nobody had the day of the robbery in Maricopa, since it wasn't a regular stop. Nobody had noticed anything like a gang of even Sunday-school teachers riding together in recent memory.

The tracks parted company with the river at Rilito to take a thirty-mile short cut across less interesting desert, passing only through three tiny desert flag stops where nobody was waving flags. At Eloy they had to stop a spell, not to let anyone on or off but to check the trestle across the flood-swollen Santa Cruz before crossing it to the west. They had to do the same thing at the smaller town of Toltec, where a side show of the river called for a smaller bridge. Then a few miles on the infernal tracks crossed back to the east bank again, scaring hell out of everybody, before scaring them some more by crossing yet another rickety trestle to the west bank again in less than fifteen miles. It served the SP right for laying its tracks more or less in line with a river that couldn't think straight. It was going on sunset when Longarm finally got off at Maricopa, where the flood-swollen waters of the Santa Rosa Wash joined the Santa Cruz to make everyone in town with a cellar worry some.

Longarm had swilled plenty of beer on the train. So after

he'd taken a leak at the depot he went directly to the local marshal's office. The old-timer on duty said you could call him Hank and that he'd been on duty the day of the robbery. He said all but one of the gang had lost the posse on the far side of the wash.

Longarm said he'd read that in the official report and asked what they'd done with the body of the one who hadn't made it. Hank said, "We buried him, of course. What do *you* do with dead bank robbers, *eat* 'em?"

Longarm chuckled and said, "Only when they look tender. I can't find nothing in my notes as to who the cuss might have been. I suspect if one of the gang could be given a handle, it might give us a better notion who he was riding with the day his luck run out. Birds of a feather do wind up with their names on the yellow sheets, you know."

The old-timer got up from behind his desk. "If the son of a bitch had even had his initials on his hatband we'd have kept a record of it," he said. "Lots of folks looked at him afore we planted him in the 'dobe. Nobody hereabouts had ever seed his puffy features afore, even on a Wanted poster. I'd strongly advise agin an exhumation order at this late date, son. He was getting sort of rancid by the time we buried him."

The old-timer opened a file drawer and took out a cigar box, adding, "We naturally kept his belongings, should someone wish to come forward for 'em. But it's a funny thing. Hardly anybody seems to know an outlaw, once he's *kilt*."

He placed the box on the desk for Longarm to go through. As he did so he asked absently how the bank robber's career had ended so abruptly. Hank said, "Pop Martin. Hardware store across from the bank. Seen 'em getting down out front, wearing rain slickers on a day as dry as a mummy's heart, and sent his errand boy for us as he loaded up his ten-gauge. They was in and out afore the boy could run two blocks, but Pop blowed that one rascal almost in half with both barrels afore he could get to his horse."

"Then at least one of their mounts was recovered?" Longarm asked.

"Not hardly. One of the *banditos* led it off as they lit out in a considerable cloud of dust. Time the rest of the town could come unstuck, they was long gone. But if old Pop Martin had only had some old boys spitting and whittling out front that day we'd be famous as Northfield, now. They say the James–Younger gang favors rain slickers, too. You reckon that's who could have done the deed?"

Longarm shook his head and said, "Doubt it. The James boys never bounced back much after Northfield and, even if they have recruited replacements by now, we're a mite far from their mama. They like to run home and hide behind her skirts between jobs. The slickers are used by lots of old boys. The idea is to keep folk from recalling just what they might have been wearing *under* the rain gear."

"I knowed that, damn it. We buried him in his slicker, by the way. Had to. Nobody offered to spring for a proper box. Don't never hold up the Maricopa bank if you want folk in town to weep at your funeral, Longarm."

Longarm rummaged through the small change, tobacco pouch, and such in the box until he found a watch of the same make as the one the rascal he'd shot to the south had been packing. He held it up to the light and shook it. It jingled and jangled a lot.

"Pop really stopped the son of a bitch's clock for him," Hank said. "Number-nine buck is sort of hard on delicate machinery. See the neat little hole in the back?"

Longarm smiled thinly and rolled the lead ball under the unbroken glass around the rim of the dial as he said, "Come right through the face, but was stopped by the glass. Must be shatterproof, or just thick enough to stop a spent shot. The hands are stuck at a quarter past three. How come?"

"How come? Why, damn it, Pop put two charges of number-nine buck into that outlaw and ever'thing he had on him, that's how come!"

"You say the hardware man saw 'em enter the bank just before closing time. He sent a runner for the law. No offense, but in a quarter of an hour I could *walk* clean through your fair city, and banks generally close at three."

Hank shrugged. "Maybe they was open a few minutes late, or they opened up when they seen customers out front," he suggested.

"Total strangers wearing rain slickers on a hot, dry afternoon? I sure wish *I* could find a bank that polite. What we got here is a mighty careless bank doorman or a bank robber who just didn't care much about the time. I'd say a gent planning to hit a bank just at closing time would be more interested in keeping good time than that, wouldn't you?"

"Oh, hell, it's a cheap watch. Could have just been set wrong."

"I know. But in that case they'd have gotten there too early, while the bank was crowded with last-minute customers. It's possible, even probable, that the one they left behind in the dust full of buckshot wasn't the leader, and the leader would be the one who'd really need to know what time it was. But I'd still better have a talk with whoever let them in. There's something here that don't smell right. Who would have been on the door somewheres around three, give or take a few minutes, Hank?"

The older lawman thought, then shrugged and said, "Beats me. Nobody would have been shutting door one if it was *earlier* than closing time. The bank guard on duty that day was old Tom Marino. He's half Mex, but a good old boy."

"You got his address, Hank?"

"He don't have no address. You just has to ask for him at the Palace Hotel. He hires furnished digs there. But I doubt old Tom will be able to tell you much. So far he's jawed with ever'one from you feds to the Arizona Rangers, and that gang's still at large. Our bank's the fourth they've helt up this year, if you're barking up the tree of an inside job. Tom Marino ain't been anywheres but Maricopa since the Apache gave him a game leg back in the Sixties."

Longarm shut the cigar box, said *adios*, and went looking for the Palace Hotel. He spied it down the main street on the far side. He moved that way, shaded by the awnings on his side of the street, and was about to cross when he saw three people coming out and stayed put. The plump man in the fancy suit and the plumper woman in an even fancier outfit were strangers to him. But if Laredo was tagging along like that, he had to be looking at Wilson Mansfield and the notorious Peggy Gordon. The banker's wife had likely been right about them having more fun earlier. On the other hand, the ass on that big bawd wasn't bad, and she sure knew how to move it as the three of them walked off down the street together. He wondered how she could move forward at all when she was moving so much from side to side. He wondered where they could be headed, too. But since adultery wasn't a federal offense, and he'd have been as guilty of it if it had been, Longarm decided talking to the bank guard made more sense right now.

He went across, entered the so-called Palace, and asked the room clerk for Tom Marino. The clerk shrugged and said, "He ain't here no more." Longarm asked if he'd left a forwarding address and the clerk replied, "Not hardly. We threw him out. He hadn't paid his rent for a month and this ain't a shelter for old, drunk cripples."

"He's been short of cash at least a month? I can see you're too generous and kindhearted for your own good, but I'm law and I got reasons for the dumb questions I ask."

"I figured you was after old Tom for some reason," the clerk said. "Some others has been by about bills he owes around town."

"How come? Don't he still have a good job at the bank?"

The clerk shrugged. "I don't know as you could call it a *good* job. But, yeah, he still works there. What Señor Tomas Marino can't seem to get through his thick head is that a man can drink and gamble or he can pay his bills. He can't do *both* on a bank guard's day wages!"

Longarm thanked him and left to hunt down the wistful-sounding old cuss. He had to ask in more than half the saloons in town. But, since the town was small, that didn't take as long as one might have expected. He caught up the gray-haired old man, who was older than Longarm had expected, in the Cactus Blossom. Marino wasn't gambling or even drinking in one corner. He'd finished his bottle of red wine, early as the night still was. Longarm asked permission and, when the old man said it was all right to join him, sat down and ordered them a couple of tumblers of red wine when the waitress gal came over to tell him nobody could just sit there without ordering. He regretted ordering wine in such unfriendly surroundings the moment she put their drinks down and said, "That'll be twenty cents."

He gave her a quarter and told her to invest the change wisely. Then he clinked glasses with the bank guard and got down to business. The old man was willing to talk. He just didn't have much to say. He said, "They just come, masked and yelling at everyone. I got under a table and stayed there till they left. You would have, too, at them odds. The damn bank expects me to stand guard with a durned old single-action .32. So I had five small-bore rounds against a dozen double-action .44s and .45s!"

"You likely done the right thing, Mr. Marino. I'm more interested in whether the door was locked or not when they hit you."

The old man stared blearily across at him and muttered, "Locked? Hell, son, they never would have got *in* if the door was locked. They come in just as I was *fixing* to lock up. But they come in afore I was even near the door to do so."

"Do you always close that door at three o'clock sharp?"

"Not exactly. The manager, Mr. Jenson, has to tell me to, first. I just work there. Jenson runs the place. He sometimes stays open a mite late if he knows an important depositor's late getting into town or, contrariwise, he's been known to have me shut the door early on a tedious hot weekday."

"Then you can't say for certain whether it was three or a little after when those robbers hit you?"

"Hell, I pawned my watch years ago, and I can't see the office clock from where I'm posted near the front. Ah, ain't you fixing to drink that wine, son?"

Longarm slid his nearly full tumbler of red ink across and said, "It don't seem to set well atop the beer I've had today. I'd be obliged if you'd finish it for me. It's been nice talking to you, Mr. Marino."

He rose, resisting the temptation to be a big shot and order Marino a bottle. For a man who helped another man kill himself an inch at a time was more like a small-time murderer.

Outside, he stood undecided, consulting his own watch under a lamppost. The timetable in his pocket said there wouldn't be another train south before ten, putting him back in Tucson around midnight. He could stay here and talk to hopefully more sober folk at the bank in the morning. On the other hand, a lot of other lawmen already had, and it hardly seemed likely anyone else had been staring too hard at their watches while they stared into a dozen gun muzzles. He was beginning to recover from that romp on the red velvet sofa enough to wonder at least a little if Gordita still liked him. He wasn't *hurting* for a woman yet, but he suspected that if he found himself alone in a fleabag hotel for the night he'd be having mighty strong hankerings to compare a little brown Mexican rump with the paler one he'd enjoyed more recently.

But the evening was young, and he didn't have to make up his mind until he saw more of Maricopa. So he started down the street to see where old Laredo and his boss had been taking that fancy gal. It had to be more luxurious than the infernal Cactus Blossom.

It was easy to discover, just by asking a townee, that the only establishment serving both ladies and gents a sporting evening, unless the lady worked there, was the Silver Sombrero Sporting Saloon. But when Longarm got there, the husky gent in the doorway said they didn't serve cowhands inside.

Longarm said, "That don't matter to me, pard. I never drink cowhands, in any case." He tried to ease past the bouncer politely, but when the son of a bitch tried to stop him he had to say flatly, "Don't try it, sonny."

The bouncer was almost as tall as Longarm and built heavier. But as he gazed into Longarm's gunmetal-gray eyes and considered how much they were paying him, he decided it wasn't enough to include sheer heroism. "Well, Blacky aint gonna like this, but I can see you look like a real big spender, so what the hell," he said.

Longarm went on in to see what all the fuss was about. He could have saved himself the tedious discussion at the front door by flashing his badge, he knew. But, for one thing, he had no real reason for being on the premises and, for another, Longarm had always disliked bullies and enjoyed calling their bluffs. A gal who read lots of books had once told him a gent who enjoyed calling bullies had a streak of bully in him, himself. But he didn't see it that way. For *somebody* had to bully bullies, and he never picked on folks who didn't deserve it.

The main salon of the saloon was crowded as well as fancy enough for a New Orleans whorehouse. Well-dressed

gents and even flashier she-males were crowded about rou-
lette and crap tables drinking from stemmed glasses as they
threw their money away and seemed to find it mighty amus-
ing for some fool reason. He moved to the bar as he gazed
about for someone he might know. He didn't see anyone.
So when the barkeep, wearing pants but pretty enough to
pose for the *Police Gazette*, asked him what his pleasure
might be, he asked how much they charged for Maryland
rye. When the sissy told him, Longarm said he was just
leaving.

He would have, too, had not an oily gent dressed all in
black with patent-leather hair to match come up to him to
say, "You have to the count of ten to make it back out on
the street where you belong, saddle tramp!"

Longarm smiled thinly and told the barkeep, "Better bring
me the whole bottle, pard. It looks like I'll be staying after
all."

The barkeep never moved to fill his order. The oily gent,
who had to be the mysterious Blacky, eyed the Colt on
Longarm's hip thoughtfully, then opened his frock coat to
clear the grips of his twin Lightnings. "What have we here,
a big bad man?" he said softly.

Longarm smiled and said, "I'm trying to be good, Blacky.
But if you want to start counting, I'll save you a dance."

Blacky said, "One!" and by the time he'd said "Two!"
the whole place got quiet as a tomb, save for one wheel
spinning down and a gal asking her escort what was going
on as he hauled her toward the door. Most of the others,
seeing they'd never make it, just got out of the line of fire.

Blacky said, "Three, and I mean it!" He might have,
too. But then some folk came out from the back room and
spoiled it all.

The two couples with Laredo just looked confused at the
frozen situation. But Laredo gasped, "Jesus!" and turned to
run like hell for the back door as Blacky stopped counting

101

long enough to frown and ask, "You know that gunslick, cowboy?"

Longarm shrugged and said, "Me and old Laredo are the victims of malicious gossip. For a time I suspicioned he was gunning for me, and now it looks like he thinks I'm gunning for him. Don't four come after three, Blacky?"

Blacky shrugged and replied, "It's my reconsidered opinion that a man who sends professional gunslicks out the back door *smiling* at them don't require a tie in here after all." He nodded at the barkeep and added, "You heard the man, Bruce. Get him his damned rye. It's on the house."

Longarm said he was much obliged as Blacky turned away and the room came back to life with a vast sigh of relief. One of the gents with Peggy Gordon and the better-looking younger gal moved closer to ask Longarm what all that had been about. "How did you put the fear of God in my bodyguard just now? I don't see any horns or a tail, and I thought I knew every important person in Tucson."

Longarm said, "I got there just as you was leaving, Mr. Mansfield. I sure hope you put the money you brought here in the other bank already. For, as you see, you don't have a bodyguard at the moment, and I ain't too sure about the wheels of fortune in this place."

The banker from Tucson frowned and asked, "Who told you about the money I was loaning the Maricopa bank, damn it?"

Longarm explained how he'd dropped by the banker's house earlier that day, leaving out the dirty parts. The banker blanched and gasped, "You know my wife? Ah, excuse us, ladies. This gent and me have to discuss private business!"

The other gent with Mansfield nodded and steered the two fancy gals across the room to a corner table as the banker asked Longarm, "Who are you, and how much do you want?"

Longarm said, "I'm Deputy U. S. Marshal Custis Long,

and I hardly ever tell a gent's wife on him unless I catch him busting federal law. Who's that other gent cheating on his wife this evening? Banker Jenson?"

"Jesus Christ! Not so loud! We're just celebrating a business deal, Long. The ladies have nothing to do with it, and I assure you the Maricopa Bank has nothing to worry about now."

Longarm said, "I want a word with Jenson anyway. About the more worrisome time he had with gents in rain slickers."

Longarm had expected Mansfield to call the younger banker over. Instead he nodded, took Longarm by the arm, and led him away from the bar as the sissy barkeep called after them, "Hey, don't you want this bottle?"

Mansfield said, "I'll introduce you to the bunch. It's understood, of course, that as a man of the world you don't mean to blab about the ladies all over Tucson?"

Longarm growled he'd already said as much as they approached the table. Young Jenson rose. The two fancy gals just stared up at Longarm as if they were two pussycats regarding a mouse wearing catnip shaving lotion.

As they joined the group, Mansfield explained who Longarm was. Miss Peggy Gordon rubbed her knee against Longarm's leg under the table as young Jenson sighed and said, "I've told the same tale to so many lawmen by now I could recite it in my sleep. Could we just go over the main points? We're keeping these little girls up past their usual bedtimes."

Longarm said, "Just spoke to your bank dick. He says he can't say just what time it was when your bank got hit."

Jenson sighed. "Here we go again! Obviously, neither can I, if you're talking about that same stopped watch. I told your treasury agents I don't watch the clock like a hawk, myself. If you want us open five or ten minutes after our usual closing time, so be it. What difference does it make?"

"If I was planning to rob a bank at closing time I'd hardly *count* on it staying open late," Longarm said. "I'd want to give myself at least five minutes leeway, lest they close *early* on me!"

"You're not the first lawman I've had this tedious discussion with. They obviously had us under observation well ahead of time and simply hit as they saw the last customers leaving, right?"

"Wrong. The hardware man across the street seen 'em ride into view in a bunch, slickered and acting determined enough for him to run for his ten-gauge. So they never shilly-shallied. They come in out of nowheres, hit, and left for the same great unknown. The one the hardware man put on the ground couldn't have been in town, let alone your bank, for anything like a quarter of an hour. Yet he departed this world well after banking hours."

"Oh, hell, his watch was fast. What do you expect from a dollar watch?"

"It could have happened that way. I've another question. About them bonds. What was government bearer bonds doing in your bank in the first place?"

"Are you serious? They were left with us for safekeeping, of course! Would you keep an unmatured bond anyone could cash in a coffee can? Our various customers who'd invested in them naturally left them in our vault for safekeeping until they were ready to be cashed."

Longarm wondered why Miss Peggy Gordon had her plump knee hooked over his own like that now, considering how innocent she looked above the table. But he wasn't talking to her as he asked, "Ain't it more usual for a bank to hold such valuables in individual safety deposit boxes, Jenson?"

The young banker flushed and said, "We don't have such facilities. I may as well confess, since you know we just had to borrow enough to keep us afloat, that our bank's not what you'd call a big financial institution."

"I didn't think you paid Tomas Marino the earth. So, in other words, you just throwed all the goodies in one safe and hoped for the best? It's no wonder they cleaned you out so good. They'd have had to work harder had each teller had his own cigar box filled with cash."

"We're installing a better vault, damn it. But I'm getting mighty tired of all this crying over spilled milk! We've borrowed enough to cover our losses, and—"

"Have you borrowed enough to cover them stolen bonds as well as the cash deposits?" Longarm cut in.

Jenson looked flustered and said, "Not exactly. But recovering government bonds is the government's business, not ours! We didn't purchase them and we didn't steal them so . . ."

"So, in other words, it's thank-you-ma'am as far as the original buyers of them bearer bonds is concerned," Longarm observed flatly. "You're covered as far as a cash run on your bank goes. But the small investors with their savings tied up in treasury paper are just out of luck because they trusted you more than them coffee cans."

"Now listen here!" The banker flushed.

But Longarm said, "No, *you* listen, you smarmy playboy! It's easy for you to sit here feeling fat-cat with the lousy twenty in cash you had to give back covered for you. But there's fifty thousand dollars' worth of little folks' savings still left over, and you're too filled with yourself to talk to us badge-toting peasants serious about it! I got to go back up the river to look for it some more. But I want you to study up and study tight on every detail of that robbery. Then I expect you to send me a written report telling me exactly where everyone on either side was standing, doing and saying what, during the entire gunpoint transaction. Send it to me care of the law in Tucson and send a copy to my boss, Marshal Billy Vail, Denver District Court, Federal

105

Building. Meanwhile, don't even *think* about foreclosing on any widows or orphans who left bonds with you for safekeeping. For, as far as I can see, *you* owe *them!*"

"I beg to differ, Deputy! My attorney assures me we can't be held accountable for anything but cash left with us for safekeeping!"

Longarm said, "Yeah, lawyers talk like that, too. I ain't a lawyer. I was brought up to know right from wrong. So you may be able to wriggle off the hook. More than one worm has in the past, and likely will in the future. So I'd best go look for them government bonds some more. I can see *you* don't give two hoots and a holler about anyone but yourself."

He had to untangle his leg from the plump whore next to him before he could rise. She looked up wistfully and said, "Don't go away mad, handsome."

"Ain't mad at *you*, ma'am," he said. "The business *you're* in is ten times more respectable than your escort's."

Chapter 7

As Longarm rode back on the night train the evaporating floodwaters had cooled the desert air so much that he regretted having left his frock coat with his other things in Tucson. But it hardly seemed likely he could freeze to death in two hours. So he found a draft-free corner in the club car and ignored the goose bumps under his shirtsleeves as he nursed a few drinks. The trip back to Tucson was less scary, partly because the floodwaters under the trestles had subsided some, but mostly because it was too dark out to see such dangers as there might be.

The train made a stop at Eloy, after crossing the Santa Cruz for the last time, around eleven. Longarm waited till they'd started up again with the usual jerk before he rose to head back to the bar, empty beer schooner in hand. He'd just put it down, telling the colored barkeep it seemed to be dead-for-the-cause again, when a dark-complected gent wearing a straw boater and a seersucker summer suit entered the club car, took one look at Longarm, and slapped leather.

He didn't make it. Longarm put him on the floor with

two rounds in his chest before he could get his .45 out from under his coattails. As he stood in the cloud of his own gunsmoke, staring soberly down at the man he'd just shot, Longarm announced, "It's all right, I'm the law." Nobody answered. The barkeep was out of sight behind the bar and the few other passengers in there with them were trying to look invisible, too.

The uniformed conductor came in from the forward cars, his own nickel-plated Detective Special ready for anything. He started to ask what was going on, recognized Longarm, and sighed, "Jesus, *that* was one short ride! He just got on at Eloy. Who was he, Longarm?"

Longarm commenced reloading as he replied, "They called him Digger Dawson. He was said to be a Paiute breed. But that wasn't why I gunned him just now. He was meaner than most Indians, or even whites, and he likely knew how often I've regarded his distinguished features on the Wanted posters. He was wanted for everything from murder and rape to purse-snatching."

Longarm put his gun away and dropped to one knee beside the late Digger Dawson to see what the dead man's pockets had to tell him. According to the I.D. in the cheap wallet, he'd just killed the wrong man. But Longarm knew the wallet was just funning. Aside from twenty-odd in cash— which would be of no value to a dead man, so five seemed more reasonable—Longarm found a slip of paper wadded up behind the fake I.D. card. He unfolded it to see it was covered with block lettering, but though the lettering was clear enough, the message wasn't. It read, "EKLOOAY BWAWNOK ATLEL SKELT FYOWR TAHOE EWNID TIHWITS MEOWNATCH." Longarm said, "You don't say," and when the conductor asked him what it said, explained, "It looks like he really must have been as Paiute as they said. 'Atl' is the word most Digger tribes use for water and, while I don't know what Tahoe means, they got a lake named

108

that up in Paiute country. The rest of it might as well be Greek until I can find me a literate Digger Indian!"

The conductor said he didn't know there were such critters. One of the other passengers who'd been listening and decided it was safe to come up from behind his table now said, "Hot damn, I'll bet *I* know what it is! They say Wovoka, the head of the Ghost Dance Cult, is an educated Paiute!"

Longarm stared thoughtfully down at the evil features of the corpse. "Maybe," he said. "This particular Paiute was half white and all bad. The Ghost Dancers are ornery, but too religious to have much truck with slime buckets like old Digger Dawson. He's always rid with white gangs up to now, and they should be ashamed of themselves. For this was one bad half-ass redskin!"

He put the mysterious message in his own wallet for now. Then he told the conductor, "There's a couple of ways we can skin this cat. You could drop him off with me at Tucson, but us federal agents ain't allowed to claim rewards, and this rascal had paper on him from everyone from Pinkerton to Wells Fargo."

The conductor stared down wistfully as Longarm added, "On the other hand, I couldn't help noticing your belly gun's a .44-40, short as it growed."

"I could easily fire it twice out the side, too. But, whilst I sure could use the money, ain't you forgetting about all these witnesses, Longarm?"

Longarm winked and said, "If *you* don't forget them, why should they tell a different tale? You *was* figuring on giving everyone here but me a cut, wasn't you?"

The conductor stared past Longarm, counting with his lips. Then he grinned. "I surely was. Least I could do for these other gents backing my play as I recognized that rascal getting on my train just now!"

There was a murmur of agreement from all around. The

barkeep put a line of shot glasses on the bar to seal the bargain as he marveled how he'd never known the old conductor was such a gunslick.

Longarm told the suddenly rich conductor, "I'd best go forward so's you can lock the door after me. One question: he got on at Eloy. Where did his ticket say he was bound for?"

"Oh, that's easy. Nogales. He asked when he got on how soon we'd get there and seemed a mite upset when I tolt him he'd have to lay over in Tucson for a day or more. Ain't he going to be surprised when we unload him in El Paso in the morning?"

"I'd drop him off sooner, if I was you. This cool spell don't figure to last much longer."

Nobody else was getting on or off when the train stopped at Tucson a little after midnight. The platform was dark and deserted. Longarm headed for the depot door and tensed some when he heard his name called softly from the pitch blackness at the far end. But he was getting used to meeting El Gato like that by now, so he strode down the planks to see what the fool Mex wanted.

El Gato said, "I have taken the *libertad* of checking you into the hotel across the street. Here is your room key. You will find your belongings in the room, of course, and the mule you admired is in the livery just down the street."

"You sure are devoted to *libertad,* old son. But how come? Have I worn my welcome out at the *posada* for some fool reason?"

"Not exactly. You were *never* welcome in the Mexican quarter, save as my guest, and my *muchachos* and me must ride for Sonora *poco tiempo*. The Yaqui are on the warpath, and my people need my protection."

"Don't Mexico have an army no more?"

"Bah! I spit in the milk of their mothers! When Yaqui

wish for to skin *Mexicano* babies just for to hear them cry, los Federales are of small comfort to their mothers. It takes *men* to fight Yaqui!"

"So I've heard. You want to have a drink with me while we talk it over?"

El Gato sat down on the platform edge. "No. I feel as welcome in this part of town as you could be made to feel in ours if word got around you no longer had friends there."

Longarm sat down beside him, reaching for some smokes as he nodded and said, "I've noticed how unfriendly some saloons can be." Then he handed El Gato a cheroot and lit it for him. "You may be able to save me a tedious trip to Nogales, seeing as you're headed that way," he added.

He brought the Mexican up-to-date on his trip to Maricopa, then asked, "Don't Yaqui talk the same Uto-Aztec dialect as Paiute, Shoshone, and such?"

"I think so. What of it?"

"Just struck me that a Paiute-speaking breed might be able to guide his pals through the Sierra Madre with a better chance of making it through alive than most. Them bonds turning up south of Texas had to get there some damn way."

El Gato shook his head. "One may *fight* his way through Yaqui country. One is not about to *talk* his way through. The Yaqui are not born conversationalists. They are the spawn of *el diablo,* at war with the rest of the human *raza.* They kill *Apache* on sight!"

"Yeah, but Apache speak Nadene, not Uto-Aztec, so *they're* strangers, too. A Digger Indian talking the same lingo might be able to reason with Yaqui."

"Reason with *hombres* raised to kill even another Yaqui if he is not from the same clan? Your Horse Utes speak the same tongue as your Diggers, no?"

"Yeah, and Horse Utes kill Paiute just for practice. I follows your drift. But there went a grand notion as might have answered many a question. Do you know any of the lingo, seeing as you must be part Aztec, no offense?"

El Gato said, "I am pure Spanish, damn it!"

Longarm chuckled. "There went another grand notion. Wait a minute. Papago are Diggers, sort of. I'll try the note I found on Digger Dawson on them, come morning."

He took a drag on his own smoke, then went on, "I'd best give you some money. Aside from what you must have put out to move me, I want you to wire me from Mexico as soon as you get a handle on what's going on down there."

El Gato looked hurt. "For why should I take money from friends when the world is filled with so many rich enemies?" he asked. "I do not need your lousy money. Not as much as you do. You do not have my freedom for to make a bank withdrawal any time you need some, eh?"

Longarm said that sounded fair. "You know what I'm interested in, to the south," he added. "A natural crook like you is in a better position to ask questions Mex crooks might not want to answer, true, to a gringo lawman. Digger Dawson was on his way to Nogales, and mayhaps further south. I'd sure like to know how come. But if the gang ain't likely to be crossing the Sierra Madre regular, they could still be using Mexico as their base of operations between bank jobs on this side of the border. They ain't been seen in the gringo parts of Nogales or, come to study on it, *anywheres* under U. S. jurisdiction, unless they're made of thin air between jobs. But the Mexican quarter down that way—"

"Not a gringo gang," El Gato cut in, going on to explain, "My *muchachos* and me make it our business to know everyone of any importance in such places. It is true a gringo can hide out in any Mex Town, if he has a Mexican for to speak up for him. But there are always those who do not like it, and there are always grumbles to be heard, no?"

"I understand why you moved me to the hotel just now. But who's to say *every* member of that gang has to be a blue-eyed blonde? The one killed in Maricopa was a gringo.

The ones doing the talking at all the robberies so far seem to have talked English natural enough. But Digger Dawson was darker than you, and if they had one or more real Mexicans riding with 'em..."

"I shall, as you say, study on it," El Gato nodded. "As I said, even one gringo in a *Mexicano* neighborhood causes talk. If a gang of them are hiding in Nogales or, God forbid, further south, I will be able to find out why, and who is protecting them."

They got up, shook on it, and parted friendly. El Gato vanished like a spook into the darkness and Longarm went first to the Western Union and then to his hotel, deciding he hadn't read Billy Vail's latest order that he come on home.

He introduced himself to the night clerk at the hotel and then bet him a dollar he couldn't be moved with his gear to another room. The clerk said he'd just lost a buck, but asked, "How come? Your Mex friend picked you out a nice corner room, Deputy Long."

"If everyone in Tucson was my friend I wouldn't be staying here tonight," Longarm said. "He's on my side. His boys are likely mostly on my side. But folk do gossip and if someone in Mex Town hadn't been making war talk, my Mex friends wouldn't have gone to so much trouble."

So the clerk helped him haul his saddle and possibles to the far corner of the second floor and, when Longarm suggested it might not be a friendly act to rent the first room to anyone else too soon, the clerk said he'd already got that part. "The place is three-quarters empty in any case, this time of the year," he added. "But how serious a visit are you expecting? I'm only paid to hand out keys, not fight off gangs of Mexicans!"

Longarm smiled soothingly. "I doubt any such gang would want to invade this part of town," he told the clerk. "I'm just being careful. By the time you've packed a badge six or eight years you sleep better in a bed nobody else knows about."

They shook on it and, when the clerk left, Longarm locked the door and braced a chair under the knob as he pondered his next move. He didn't have too many choices this late at night. He knew it would be safe to pay a call on Lila Mansfield, but he'd told her husband he wouldn't mention who he'd seen him with in Maricopa, and he knew the fool woman would try to get it out of him. Gordita was out, likely for good. Knowing her people, Longarm suspected that she was the cause of his current unpopularity. Womankind caused nine out of ten fights between his kind and Gordita's. He'd have known not to mess with a Mex gal had not a Mex fixed him up with her.

Calling on Erica Frankenberg at this hour would just be silly. So that left going to bed alone. He'd done it before and so far it hadn't killed him. But he didn't know until his head hit the pillow how bone-tired he really was. He dropped off at once and never stirred until he opened his eyes to see it was broad day and he was hungry as a wolf.

He got up, whore-bathed and dressed, and couldn't believe it was so late when he finally checked the time. It was small wonder he was so hungry. It was almost nine o'clock.

He went downstairs and found a beanery. It was surprisingly cool for Tucson. The flood of the day before had all dried out as far as the eye could see, of course, but the air needed time to heat up again. So it likely wouldn't become unbearable again this side of noon.

Once he'd eaten and coffeed himself wide awake, Longarm toted his gear to the nearby livery and saddled the frisky Spanish mule to ride out to the Double B. It was hard to keep his mouth from singing and dancing on such a beautiful morning. The desert pavement around them already looked dry and dusty as ever, but the mule left sharp hoofprints in the trail and as they passed a tall saguaro he noted the dumb

114

vegetable had drunk itself to bursting in the unexpected cloudburst and was split from the roots up like a sliced-open watermelon. It would likely die. It hardly seemed fair, since it took a saguaro a hundred years or more to grow up. Now all it was good for, since the saguaro was one of the few cactus plants with a woody inside, was a day's worth of piss-poor firewood once it finished drying out. Most of the other saguaros they passed had made it through the rain, and the prickly pears looked fat and sassy, while cactus wrens chirped and lizards scampered in the open after ants, enjoying the rare chance for a morning stroll across what was usually a stove-top by now.

Nobody seemed to be tailing him this time, but as he read the sign ahead he saw at least one buckboard was preceding him along the trail. It had left town an hour or more earlier, judging by the edges of the wheel marks.

He found the buckboard in front of the ranch house when he got to the Double B. Erica Frankenberg came out on the veranda with little Willy May to greet him as he rode in, so he knew whose buckboard it was. He dismounted and said, "Morning, ladies. Where's the Indians?"

Willy May explained that they were camped just up-stream, behind a nearby clump of willow. He tethered the mule and said he'd best have a word with them first. So the women went back inside as he strode into the bushes, taking out the note he'd found on the late Digger Dawson.

The old man greeted him warmly, and this time some of the kids even came out of the shelters to stare shyly at a white man closer in. Longarm knew he'd only scare the lights out of them if he paid any attention to them, so he just hunkered down beside the old Papago and asked him if he knew how to read. The Indian looked at him as if he was drunk. "I'll see if I can read this aloud to you, then," Longarm said.

It didn't work. The old man brightened at one or two

115

words, or sounds, but when Longarm had finished, he said, "Not Papago. Maybe Ho. Real People. But if a real person wrote that, he spoke funny, for a Ho."

"Well, I could be pronouncing it even funnier, and it stands to reason Paiute wouldn't say every word the same as a Papago. American English and English English don't sound exactly the same, though we do manage to follow each other's drift if we listen sharp."

He read it again. The old man shook his head, then called out in a lingo that sounded a lot the same and, when an old woman came out of one hut, not looking at Longarm, the old Papago said, "This one used to be Paiute before I captured her. Read that again to her."

Longarm did. The old woman seemed to ignore him, but when he'd finished she mumbled something to the old man, who said, "She says there is a Paiute band known as the Ta. So Tahoe means the Ta People. But she says the other words mean nothing to her. She says maybe it could be Shasta or Washo. They live west of the Paiute in the Sierra Nevada, and she says they talk funny. I don't know. I have never been that far north."

Longarm put the note away and asked the old man to thank her. He didn't, but the old woman ducked back inside anyway. Longarm said, half to himself, "A renegade breed could have been from some Sierra Nevada tribe or, hell, Eskimo, for all we really know of his mysterious past. I got another favor to ask, Chief."

"Name it. This is a good place to camp. We are happy here. Our women enjoy the iron water pumps, and last night the young woman who lives in the house gave us coffee."

"I told you she was a good person," Longarm said. "That heavy rain may have brought signs of digging to the surface. If your young men looked, they might be able to see where anything or anyone was buried recent on this spread."

The old man nodded and said he'd have them scout for

sign. Longarm got up and returned to the house. The two gals served him coffee and cake in the parlor as he brought them up-to-date on the little he'd found out about Willy May's late brother, adding, "It's starting to look like old Bucky was an innocent dupe, not a member of any gang."

The teen-aged blonde thanked him for his words of cheer. The older blonde said, "Thank heavens. For, as I was just explaining to the child when you rode in, Judge Watson has agreed to hurry probate provided I can assure him no criminal charges are likely to come up to cloud the estate. He's even agreed to appoint me Willy May's guardian until she's of age, the old dear. I confess I was more than surprised. Judge Watson is such a gruff, growly bear in court that I never would have expected him to say he thought I was at least as smart as the last three men he hanged. I think he meant that as a compliment. I was sure he'd be prejudiced against me as a mere woman."

Longarm frowned. "There you go again with that 'mere woman' stuff again. No offense, but it seems to me that if anyone's showing prejudice it's *you*, Miss Erica. Do you know for a fact your Judge Watson is a wife-beater or a white slaver? You say he's hanged at least three *men* in recent memory. How many *she-males* has he sent to the gallows that you know of?"

She dimpled and said, *"Touché.* But I was still surprised to find a gruff old frontier judge so willing to take a she-male, as you put it, so seriously."

"How come? You're a qualified attorney and you talk sensible about most everything but the war between sexes, which my sex never declared in the first place."

"That's not true!" she declared with a considerable scowl. "It's a man's world. We girls get the short end, and you know it!"

Longarm shrugged. "I ain't sure I'd have chose to be a she-male, had I been consulted about it before I was birthed.

117

But I wasn't, and neither was you. So here we are, and I reckon we just have to make the best of it. There's advantages to being a he and there's others to being a she. But if you don't like the deal the Lord cut with you, why don't you take it up with the management? Not even your daddy could be accused of fathering you as a daughter instead of a son, or a hunting dog he might have had more use for. I've talked about women to many a man, including some who'd shock you when it came to holding she-brains in low repute. But to date I've yet to meet a man who chortled with glee about the way he'd personally set things up so's his wife would have a headache at times he was feeling more friendly. You're picking on innocent bystanders, Miss Erica. Us *men* didn't do nothing to you."

"All right. But you can't say you don't take advantage of the deal we got from the Lord, can you?"

"Nope. It's human nature to take advantage. Big-shot men take advantage of little-shot men, as well as anyone else they can get the Indian sign on. Rich ladies take advantage of their maids. If a big schoolgirl gets mad at a *little* schoolgirl, guess who wins eight out of ten times?"

Before the discussion could get any sillier, the old Papago banged on the door and called out, "Longarm! Hear me, we have found something!"

Longarm excused himself and went out to find out what it was. The old man led him around to the far side of the fenced-in horses, where some other Papago were staring down at a patch of soil a mite darker than it should have been this long after a heavy rain. Longarm nodded and said, "Yep, that soil's been disturbed within the last year or so. Let's dig her up."

The Digger Indians went to work with the digging sticks they'd carried since they were old enough to walk, and in no time at all they had a green-painted strongbox out of the shallow hole. Longarm told everyone to stand back as he shot the lock off. Then he opened it and muttered, "Shit." For the strongbox was empty.

He was standing there wondering why when Erica ran up to him, saying she'd just heard a shot. "I know," he said. "We was just opening this box. It's the sort of box they carry valuables in, and somebody buried her here like a pirate treasure. But, as you can see, they went to a lot of trouble for a treasure trove of pure air!"

She said, "Oh, it must be evidence they wanted to hide!"

"Evidence of what?" he replied.

"Couldn't the stolen bonds have been stored in a special way?" she asked.

He started to shake his head, then changed his mind. "Good thinking. I'd best find out. For the notes they gave me never said, and it does make sense that such valuable paper wouldn't just be scattered across the bottom of a bank safe. I've got to go back to town and wire the bank in Maricopa. Praise the Lord for small favors, they never took nothing but *money* from any *other* bank!"

Longarm thanked the Indians and, as they walked back to the house, Erica said her business here was finished for now, so they agreed to keep each other company back to town. Little Willy May kissed them both goodbye, for some fool reason. Then they were on their way, with Erica driving her buckboard and Longarm seated beside her, with the mule tethered behind.

She'd seemed to enjoy the notion of his company to begin with, since it had been her notion in the first place. But once they were on the desert alone she seemed to grow pensive, for some reason. Longarm glanced up at the clear cobalt sky and asked, "What's the matter? It ain't that hot yet."

"As a matter of fact, it's a lovely day for this time of the year," she said. "I was just thinking about the argument we had back there."

"We wasn't having no argument, ma'am. We was just discussing plain facts. But do we have to start up with 'em again? Like you said, it's a nice day, the birds are chirping sweet, and I don't want to chirp no more about how often I leaves women beaten half to death in dark, dank caves."

She laughed. "I've heard about the condition you leave some women in, Custis. I fear Judge Watson is an old gossip as well as an old dear, and you seem to have quite a reputation in legal circles."

"Do tell! I don't know Judge Watson, so I just can't tell you how wicked *he* may or may not be with the ladies. I ain't never been wickeder than any lady I've met up with. So you don't have to worry about me throwing you down in a clump of prickly pear, if that's what's eating you."

She sighed. "Judge Watson said you were said to be decent, as a matter of fact. He said a lady like me had nothing to fear from a man like you, and to pay no mind if you talked a mite dirty."

Longarm frowned. "I ain't talking dirty. But you and that old busybody sound like a couple of kids asking one another what that word on the outhouse wall really means. Respectable folk sure give me a pain."

They rode on in silence for a time. Then Erica asked, "Doesn't it bother you to...well...love 'em and leave 'em, Custis?"

He shrugged. "Not as much as never getting no loving at all, I reckon. It ain't that I'm heartless. At times I've felt mighty wistful about riding on, as a matter of fact. But, as you might have noticed, I pack a badge. A man in my line of work makes enemies. So I'd hate to leave a pretty young widow weeping for me and, since I hardly want to settle down with an *old* and *ugly* gal, I don't mean to settle with *any* before I hang up my guns for keeps."

"In other words, your career comes first?"

"Don't know if you could call what I do a *career*. Sometimes it can get to be a dirty *job*. But that's about the size of it. I won't be too old to look at women when they put me out to pasture with my pension. So, meanwhile, it's best not to get too close to any gal in particular."

"I can understand that," she sighed. "I've had to put my own career ahead of personal longings. But it's different for a *man*. You can enjoy a carefree fling now and then. A woman can't."

"How come? Do you have to announce it to the newspapers every time you get kissed, Miss Erica?"

She called him a big goof and added, in a sadder voice, "In a town as small as Tucson, a lady doesn't *have* to announce it to the newspapers, or even to her neighbors. They just *know*. I confess I've considered what might happen if I could meet a *very* discreet single man. But it would probably be so much work I'd never get my real work done."

"Don't do it, then. You pure gals may not know it, but sneaky kisses are sort of like peanuts. It's hard to stop at one or two after you've got used to the taste. You're better off riding alone till you meet some gent worth introducing to the neighbors, open."

She sighed again and said, "I know. I fear I know what peanuts taste like, too, thanks to a silly summer I spent one vacation from law school in my sadly unshady past. But I fear I'm just not meant to have secret lovers, and I'm sure not ready to marry yet."

He didn't answer. They rode on quite a ways before she said almost to herself, "God, I wish I were a man. But *one* of these days, if I ever get my nerve up, I surely mean to have one rip-snorting romance before I die!"

He smiled thinly. "*Before* you die, Miss Erica? You'll play hell having anything *after* you die."

She laughed. "I wish you hadn't reminded me of that.

It's not the first time that occurred to me, you know."

"Didn't think you was dumb. So, all right, do you want to get laid, Miss Erica?"

She gasped, reined in, and slapped him across the face, ordering him to get out before she screamed. He didn't want her scaring the cactus wrens out here in the middle of nowhere with her screaming, so he got down and went around to untether his mule as she called after him, "I'm sorry, Custis. I had no call to do that after saying things that might have given any man the wrong idea about me."

He mounted up and reached for a smoke as he said, "I reckon I understand you better than you do, Miss Erica. So I'd best just ride on in ahead, and we'll say no more about it, hear?"

As he heeled the mule forward she yelled, "Wait! If you find anything out about that strongbox, you know where to find me, and it's my right to know!"

He didn't answer. He just rode on as she started up behind him. He knew she had some rights, should he find out anything involving her client at the Double B. He sure hoped he wouldn't. For if there was anything he hated worse than a gal who teased, right now he couldn't think what it might be.

Chapter 8

When he got back to town, Longarm stabled the mule and sent a wire to the bank in Maricopa. Then he went across to the nearest saloon to give Banker Jenson time to answer. It wasn't noon yet, so the place was empty, save for him and the barkeep. Longarm ordered needled beer and carried it to a corner table to nurse. He was halfway down the schooner and fixing to get up and go back to the Western Union when the batwing doors swung open and a gent he'd never seen before came in, wearing nothing of any great interest save for a buscadero gunbelt carrying a brace of ivory-handled Colt .74, low on each hip. The stranger walked sort of feline as he came direct to Longarm's corner, smiled down as friendly as a pumpkin on Halloween night, and said, "If you'd be Longarm, I'm looking for you. They said you come in here just now."

"You come to the right place," Longarm said. "What can I do for you?"

"They call me Bounty Breslin. No doubt you've heard of me?"

"I have. I'd offer to shake, but I just washed my hands. Fortunately for you, the men you've killed for hire, so far, has been covered by your private investigator's license. Who might you be after now, Bounty?"

The hired gun shifted his weight. "You," he said. "But could we step out back to have it out? It's always so much neater if the winner don't have to worry about witnesses when he explains it was self-defense."

Longarm laughed incredulously. "Hold on, old son. Not even the hunting license you bought off that judge who ought to be ashamed of himself could possibly cover a *federal deputy!*"

"Why not? You sure *look* like a bail-jumper I got on my list, sort of. How was I to know, when you slapped leather on me, that you was just suffering righteous indignation?"

"We'd best study on this, Bounty. Care for a beer? Never mind. I see we seem to have the place all to ourselves at the moment. Ain't it amazing how shy guns make barkeeps?"

"Yeah, I've noticed how few gents like to be calt as witnesses. You want to step out back or do you want it here, Longarm?"

Longarm said, "I ain't through with my beer yet, and since the clock on the wall says your noonday train won't be leaving in less'n ten minutes we got plenty of time, Bounty. Do you mind telling me what this is all about? It won't matter to you one way or the other, after, no matter who wins."

Breslin grinned crookedly. "They told me you was cool. Told me you was *good,* too," he said. "So, all right, I'll extend you professional courtesy. I'm getting a flat five thousand for the job. I hope you finds that flattersome."

"I do, knowing you'd shoot your mother in the back for a nickel, Bounty. Would you mind telling me who finds my continued existence so distasteful?"

"You're just stalling. I'm offering you a fair fight. But you're right about that train, and we ain't got time for a long conversation. So if you don't want to try, you'll just have to die with your fool hands on the table like that. For you know you can't draw worth a damn, sitting down."

"That's why I ain't making sudden moves, of course. You're figuring to slap leather as I start to get up, right?"

"Hell, I'll give you an even break, old son. I know for a fact no man born of mortal woman can beat me to the draw. So I likes to make it interesting."

"I heard you was a man who loved your work, Bounty. Train won't be here for a good five minutes or more and you know how gunplay draws flies. You was about to tell me who sent you after me, remember?"

"*I'm* calling the shots here, you grinning bastard!" snapped the hired gun. He added almost plaintively, "What's the matter with you, Longarm? Can't you see your remaining life is numbered in minutes?"

"Well, I never figured on living forever, Bounty. Are you afraid to tell me who sent you? You sure don't look like a man who's planning on losing when he goes for them pretty guns."

Bounty Breslin might have told Longarm, had not they both heard a train whistle mourning outside.

"It's been nice talking to you, Longarm," Breslin said. So Longarm decided he'd better fire first, and did so. Twice.

The hired killer staggered back, fighting for balance and breath with two rounds in his chest as Longarm kicked the table between them out of the way and rose, hauling out his bigger gun. Bounty Breslin dropped the derringer *he'd* been holding palmed and followed it to the sawdust with a sad little sigh.

Longarm strode over, kicked the belly gun well clear, and hunkered down to ask Bounty how he was feeling. The professional stared through him at a pressed tin ceiling he couldn't see either and asked numbly, "How did you *do* that, Longarm?"

Longarm said, "Same way you meant to do me, old son. I told you I knew your rep. So I knew from the start them single-action fancies you displayed to the world was meant for greenhorns to keep an eye on as you killed 'em sneaky. So I was watching your cupped right fist all the time you was trying to goad me into a foolish move. I'd show you the derringer I was palming on you all the time as well, but your eyes look sort of cloudy. Can you still hear me, you sneaky son of a bitch?"

"Go to hell," muttered the dying man.

"Save me a seat, Bounty," Longarm said. "But before you give my regards to the boys down there, who sent you after me?"

Bounty Breslin told Longarm to do something that was not only physically impossible but sounded painful. Then he died. Longarm got to his feet just as Marshal Cunningham tore through the batwings, looking excited about something.

Longarm said, "That's the wrong way to run into a saloon after hearing gunshots, old son. What you heard was this derringer I'd best reload now. What I shot was a no-good bounty hunter called Breslin. I'll sign the papers, but there's no sense keeping him on ice, for there ain't a soul I know of who'd want him shipped home for burial."

"Well, we can't leave anything that disgusting on the city dump, lest Tucson get a name for untidy habits," Cunningham said. "So we'll plant him in potter's field, I reckon. But how come a bounty hunter was after *you*, Longarm?"

"He mentioned a considerable sum, so he must have thought it covered the stretching of the usual rules. It sure would have simplified things if I'd been able to get him to tell me who finds me so valuable. But when I saw his hand move I had to move mine, damn it."

Cunningham stared morosely down at the corpse. "He

must have been *loco en la cabeza,* slapping leather on a man of your rep."

"He never slapped leather, fair, on anyone," Longarm said. "That's how he got his own rep. It was an old dodge I've run into before. That's how come I'm still working on getting old."

The barkeep came back in, looking sheepish. Longarm just looked disgusted as he said, "We'll have this mess off your floor in a minute, pard. Cunningham, could you see to the sordid details for me? I got to see if Maricopa's answered a wire yet."

The town law said he'd be proud to and that Longarm would find the coroner's report to sign later in the day when he got around to it. Longarm left as the saloon started to fill up. He went back to the Western Union and, sure enough, Banker Jenson had wired back that the stolen bonds had indeed been in an old Wells Fargo strongbox, painted green. He also wanted to know why Longarm was asking, but Longarm wasn't ready to tell anyone yet. For one thing, someone had gone to the trouble of putting a new padlock on the box before burying it shallow enough to be found by serious searchers, as well as empty. It was looking more and more as if someone was out to make the boy they'd used as a dupe, and then killed, guilty of more than just being foolish. He'd figure out why as soon as he figured out what the hell they wanted the law to suspect the late Bucky Bronson of being.

The murdered boy didn't work as a gang member who'd double-crossed the leader with one tedious little bond. It was supposed to look that way, he could see. By leaving the useless, empty strongbox at the Double B they'd tried to feed him a put-together. Sure, it looked as if someone might have left bonds buried there for safekeeping until they cooled off. It looked as if the young horse breeder they'd taken into their confidence could have helped himself to just one for, say, drinking money and been gunned for being so stupid. But if the bonds were being redeemed in Mexico, there wouldn't have been any at the Double B for Bucky to steal, and his sister had said two of the gang members had asked him to go into town with them. Why? To cash one small bond, dangerous, or to leave a red herring for the law to sniff at?

As Longarm came out of the Western Union Erica was waiting for him on the walk. She gasped, "I just heard you were in another shootout! Oh, Custis, I was so worried!"

He said, "So was I. Could we find someplace more shady to talk? I got a little news to tell you about the Bronson kids."

He expected her to lead him to her office, but she said her own digs were closer.

Erica Frankenberg lived alone in a small 'dobe halfway between the depot and her more imposing place of business. The inside walls were whitewashed and the floor was tiled with bricks set in sand. The tiny place was clean and likely big enough for one person. But it was all one room, with the kitchen hearth at one end and a sort of imposing bedstead made up as a sofa at the other. Erica sat him down and said she'd put some coffee on, but he told her he'd already had enough to keep him awake for a month. So she sat beside him as he got rid of his hat and explained, "They left that empty strongbox out to the Double B to be found as soon as anyone got around to suspecting Bucky Bronson. They duped him into cashing one bond so's he'd be a suspect, not knowing how dumb the law can be at times. What we got here is a ringleader who admires tricky chess when, most of the time, life's just tedious checkers. He must read a lot."

She said, "I can see how they meant to frame the poor innocent boy."

"He wasn't innocent *total*," Longarm said. "You can't

cheat an honest man, as the saying goes, and it's true enough. Bucky was as easy to tempt as most poor boys. He just didn't know what he was getting into. He swapped mounts without seeing fit to report it. He cashed a bearer bond he had no right to, likely because they offered him that five dollars and he didn't really care where they might or might not have gotten it. Then they killed him, knowing that sooner or later the bond would be traced to him. Since he's dead and his sister's innocent as driven snow, I see no call to put that in my official report, of course."

"But don't you have to report the recovered strongbox, Custis?"

He shrugged. "Sure. But everybody knows the skunks rid off with it and it had to turn up someplace. I don't think they carried it all the way here *full*. I think they divided the loot not far from Maricopa and split up. Not more than two or three rode for Tucson, for that's all I can count in these parts. The others scattered Lord knows where. For if I *knew,* I'd be able to *catch* 'em! It seems obvious they split up between jobs. And, oh, do you savvy any Indian lingo?"

"Good Lord, no! My folk were *German* immigrants!"

"Didn't think Frankenberger was a Sioux name. But it was worth a try. I don't know for sure if the late Digger Dawson was a member of the same gang or just out looking for trouble on his own. But I sure wish I could read his writing better."

"How do you know it's Indian, and not some sort of secret code?" she asked. He started to say there were Indian words mixed in with the gibberish. But then he remembered the only Indians around here seemed to find it Greek to them as well and got it out, asking, "Is there something around here I could put this note down on to pencil some?"

She turned and said, "Use my back." So he did, spreading the paper on her back and using his pencil stub gently lest he bruise her soft flesh as he said, "They taught us simple ciphers in the army. I'll start with the one everyone knows."

A few minutes later he said, "Son of a bitch! Sorry, ma'am!"

She asked what was wrong and he said, "Look what happens when you cross out every other letter."

She took the note and read, "ELOY BANK ALL SET FOR THE END THIS MONTH." Then she gasped and said, "Custis! That's *today!*"

He got to his feet as he said, "I noticed, and the only damn train south this side of three left at noon! Excuse me, ma'am. I got some tracks to make!"

As he dashed out, she called after him to come back and tell her as soon as he knew anything. He just started running, firing his .44 in the air for attention as he headed for the Western Union.

Naturally, he had company by the time he got there. Marshal Cunningham fell in step beside him to ask what was going on.

"The Eloy bank's next," Longarm snapped. "Is there any way we can get a posse there this side of three?"

Cunningham gasped. "Hell, no, it's a good fifty miles across open desert! Who told you they mean to rob the Eloy bank, Longarm?"

"Never mind that right now. Got to at least warn the law downstream!"

They ran into the Western Union office together, trailed by a couple of Cunningham's deputies by now. Longarm grabbed a blank and scribbled fast as he told the bemused clerk on duty, "You get this message to Eloy fast, and to hell with any ahead of it, hear?"

The clerk scanned the message, whistled softly, and ran for his sending key as Longarm turned to Cunningham. "Reckon they'd have a hand-cart over to the railyards?" he asked.

Cunningham shook his head. "I know for a fact they

130

don't, and you'd look silly as hell trying to pump fifty miles in less than two and a quarter hours anyway!"

Longarm smiled sheepishly and said, "When you're right, you're right. But I'm so mad at myself right now, I could spit. For I carried that message to the ringleader all night, and...Wait a minute. The message never got *through!* I ventilated the bearer of such tidings long before he could have hoped to reach Nogales, and...When's the next train to Nogales? I got the timetable here some damned wheres."

He'd just gotten it out when Cunningham said, "Ain't no train *going* to Nogales today, Longarm."

Longarm scanned his timetable. "Yep. You and the SP seem to be in total agreement on that. But Digger Dawson told the conductor he was bound for Nogales, and...Never mind, he always was a sneaky son of a bitch. He meant to get off here in Tucson, I reckon."

"Hot damn! That must mean at least one member of the gang's holed up right here, and if he's the ringleader——"

"Hold the thought," Longarm cut in. "We'll know directly whether Dawson was carrying that message to or *from* their boss. They've cased the bank in Eloy and figured another sneaky exit, or they wouldn't have been sending messages nowheres. But I know for a fact that one gang member who used to be in Tucson is dead, for I killed him myself."

"You mean Bounty Breslin?"

"Nope. The one as tried to jump me on the desert south of town. Breslin was a hired assassin, not a bank robber."

"But he must have been in on it with the gents you're after, right?"

"He never said. He might have been sent by the gang leader to shut me away for keeps. On the other hand, I'm after lots of folk and, up to now, they've got me so *confused* you'd think they'd want me *alive!* Have you ever tried to put a puzzle together when you have too many pieces?"

"Sure. I only solves about half my cases, same as any other lawman. But the gent who tried to gun you out on the desert must have been a member of the gang, and the late Bucky Bronson can tell you for sure they're killers."

Longarm lit a smoke and called back to the telegraph clerk, asking him how he was doing. The clerk called back, "The Eloy law says it's much obliged, and that anyone hitting the bank this afternoon will figure they're back at Shiloh!"

Cunningham chuckled. "That does her, then. You warned 'em in time, Longarm."

"I hope so," Longarm said. "I feel so damned *useless,* just moping about fifty miles from where I'm *supposed* to be, damn it!"

"Don't be such a show-off," the older lawman said. "I know the boys down the line in Eloy, and they're good. It ain't fair to hog *all* the owlhoots to yourself, son. Let someone else have the fun once in a while."

Longarm smiled sheepishly and allowed Cunningham was right. So they shook on it and parted, each to kill the next few itchy hours as best he could.

Longarm didn't think he'd best go back to Erica's just yet. He had to be back at the telegraph office no matter how things turned out at the lawyer gal's. Drinking on duty for two whole hours sounded even dumber, so he went back to his hotel.

The day clerk on duty said, "A gent was by here looking for you earlier. His name was Breslin, I think."

"He found me," Longarm said. "Is there any way to get a real bath around here without jumping in the Santa Cruz? I admire the sink upstairs, but I ain't had a real bath in a coon's age."

The clerk chuckled and told him the water in the bath house out back was likely a mite cleaner as well as even warmer than the river. Longarm went upstairs, got his hotel towel and a clean shirt and underwear from his possibles roll, and enjoyed a long, hot soak, changing the water a couple of times once he saw how disgusting he'd gotten since Denver.

After he'd bathed and thrown away his old socks and such, Longarm found a barber open and got to read two back issues of the *Police Gazette* before it was his turn. He was richer than usual, thanks to recent meetings with gents who didn't need their pocket money no more, so he had the barber give him a shave as well as the haircut he really needed. When the barber said there was no extra charge for bay rum Longarm told him to go ahead and stink him pretty. He still had a quarter of an hour to kill when he finally came out, cleaner that usual but still feeling dirty for some reason. He knew he was wasting his time on that she-male lawyer and that Gordita was off limits. So he ate a bowl of chili across from the Western Union as he forced himself not to be a pest and, at a quarter after three, went on across to see what had happened down the line at Eloy.

Nothing had, and the Eloy law was mad as hell about it, judging from the rude wire they'd just sent him. As he turned to leave, Marshal Cunningham came in, asking, "Well?"

Longarm said, *Nada*. They was either waiting on that coded message, or they found out about Dawson and guessed how smart I was."

"At least they didn't rob the bank this afternoon, thanks to you either way," Cunningham said.

Longarm smiled thinly. "Tell 'em that in Eloy. They've been staked out in the sun a spell and ain't cooled off yet. Are you sure there's no sudden way to get from here to Nogales?"

"Not by rail, and it's a two-day ride by horse. Why?"

"Thought Dawson might have meant to wire Nogales from here last night. But that don't work, neither. Even if

133

trains run more regular hereabouts, they were cutting it mighty fine, putting out the word less'n a day before the bank job was planned. They just can't be hiding out that far south between jobs. They can't be holed up in Mex Town here in Tucson. So what's left?"

"Not a dozen strangers here in the white part of town. Not in a bunch. I'd know."

"What if they was staying here, there, and everywhere?"

"I'll have my boys ask around. It ain't like Tucson was a big city, you know. There's only a few hotels and boarding houses, and strangers staying in a private house draws comment from the neighbors. I can see one or two hiding out here discreet. But if there's a *dozen* of the cockroaches, they sure don't come out in the light worth mention!"

Longarm sent another wire, as a long shot, to the Southern Pacific. When Cunningham asked why, he said, "Innocent bystanders aboard that train last night would have wanted their split on the late Digger Dawson."

Cunningham nodded sagely. "I follow your drift. There's no natural law saying that train could only carry one gang member at a time, and a sneak would naturally have told the others of your interest in the scout's message. You sure think good on your feet, Longarm."

The younger lawman sighed. "I wish I thought *better*. For, as of the moment, I'm pure stuck."

"Ready to give up?"

"Nope. I'm seldom *that* stuck, no matter what the home office says."

Chapter 9

When he went back to Erica's he couldn't help noticing she smelled like she'd had a bath and put on some stink-pretty since last they'd sat on her bed together. But he didn't comment, and she didn't mention his bay rum. He brought her up-to-date on the little he knew now. Erica said she was just as puzzled as ever and asked what he meant to do next.

Longarm said, "Ain't sure. All the arrows point here to Tucson or further *south*. So I reckon I'd best head *north*, next."

"But why?" she gasped. "If they called off the robbery in Eloy they could be anywhere. And even I can see they have to have been in Mexico at least once recently."

He shook his head. "That's what they want everyone to think," he said, "but it won't work. The Mexican officials to the south don't like even honest *Americanos*, and the Yaqui hate everybody. So there's no way anyone made her across to central Mexico in a bunch without leaving a trail of gunsmoke. One or two might have made it, not no gang.

135

And even if gangs were free to come and go as they liked in the Sierra Madre, it's too infernal *far!* They been hitting up and down the Santa Cruz, not more than a few days' ride apart. Digger Dawson cased the bank for 'em in this neck of the woods, so they have to be hiding out somewhere in this neck of the woods between jobs. They *want* me to think they crossed the line at Nogales. So they never."

"But, Custis, didn't they cash a bond in Nogales?" she protested.

"That's what I just said. One small amount, like they did here, to drag a red herring across my nose. They didn't do any serious cashing until they got the bonds into Mexico, likely by mail or a solo messenger like Dawson. *One* man can go most anywhere. But if the whole gang rode off to Mexico after the Maricopa job, they wouldn't have been planning to hit Eloy this very afternoon."

She said, "I give up. Nothing about this case of yours makes sense." Then, as he started to rise, she added, "Where do you think you're going?"

He settled back beside her. "Ain't sure. But a man has to be someplace. Don't you have to get back to your office now that siesta time is over?"

"I suppose I should, but I've been thinking and thinking about what you said earlier, about making up for lost time after we're dead. We lead such mayfly lives, Custis. Do you know I'm almost thirty and, up to now, I've only made love seven times in my entire life?"

He raised an eyebrow at her and asked, "Do you keep score?"

She blushed and looked away. "When it's only been that often you still do," she said. "The last time a man even kissed me was over five years ago."

He said that hardly seemed fair and hauled her in to kiss her good. She kissed back passionately, and with considerable skill if she'd been telling the truth. But when they came up for air she gasped, "Wait. Before we go any further, you promise you'll never *tell?*"

He said, "Sure I will. I always take out a broadside in the *Denver Post* to tell the world I've just kissed a pretty she-male!"

She called him a big goof, and this time *she* hauled *him* in for the kiss. So he lay her back across the bed covers and got to work on her buttons as she sighed and said, "Oh, well, as long as they only hear about this in Denver..."

They got to know one another a lot better right away. He undressed quickly while she pleaded, "Hurry! Hurry! Don't tease me so, you brute!"

Then, as he mounted her nude blonde body to soothe her nerves with a friendly injection she moaned way too loud for a lady trying to be discreet and almost shouted, "Yessss! Oh, Jesus! I'd forgotten how good it felt, and I've been abusing myself too much for my own health, trying to remember!"

So he screwed her good, making her come twice ahead of him before he shot in her the way she begged for it. "Oh, I felt that! Can we do it again with a pillow under me, darling?" she gasped.

He said he was game for *two* pillows, and she laughed like hell as he suited deeds to words. But as he entered her again in a sort of startling position, she got to moaning and groaning again and warning him she'd kill him if he didn't spend the whole night with her. He allowed he had no better place to go right now as he got in her even deeper. But after they'd made love for an hour or so she said screwing made her hungry and got up to fix them some grub as he admired her from the bed. She looked mighty handsome frying eggs naked as a jay, save for a tiny calico apron she slipped on to keep from spattering the parts he liked most about her with hot grease.

They ate sitting on the bed together, then had each other

137

some more for dessert. But the trouble with the best of times was that they tended to run down with the clock and so, by the time they'd settled down to just smoking and cuddling on her rumpled bed, the sun was barely setting outside. She noticed and said, "Damn. We're going to have to think of some new positions if I mean to keep you here all night!"

He chuckled, patted her smooth rump as she nestled her blonde head on his bare shoulder, and said, "This ain't an athletic contest, honey. Sometimes I think just petting and talking, after, can be the best part."

"Are you saying I'm a lousy lay, you brute?"

"Honey, if you was any better, I'd never survive a night with you. But if I mean to, we'd best learn to pace ourselves. Haven't you ever . . . well . . . sort of shacked up with a gent before?"

She said, "I wish you wouldn't put it so crudely. Of course you know I'm no virgin. But hitherto it's always been . . . you know . . . sort of unexpected in a carriage or on a picnic blanket. I was so mortified when you started to actually *undress* me, way back when. But you're right, it does seem ever so much nicer and, somehow, *cleaner* this way. I don't mind you seeing my body at all, now. Now that you've explored it so, I mean."

She started to explore him some more with one hand. "Hold it," he said. "Not *that*, damn it. There's no need to be in such a hurry, unless you're expecting a husband you never told me about home soon."

She giggled. "What a dirty mind you have, bless you. I guess I'm just not used to this afterwards business. I mean, I've heard about all sorts of things people do to each other in bed, but nobody ever told me a joke about just *chatting*, naked and clinging together like this."

"That's because there's nothing wicked enough to make up jokes about, once a man and woman get over their first frantic shyness. Don't it feel nice, though, just lying here like pals?"

She snuggled closer and said, "Oh, yes, heavenly. But I still feel a little awkward. I mean, what on earth are two naked people supposed to talk about, if it's not wicked?"

"Anything. They say the only time anyone's really sane, total, is right after a good warm meal and a good hot screwing. The rest of the time we all got other things in the backs of our head."

She thought for a moment. "I do feel terribly sane right now," she agreed. "What topic of discussion shall I suggest? Should we talk about your case some more?"

He grimaced. "Not hardly. I've found that once I've run out of answers and catch myself just chasing my own tail to nowheres, it's best to drop it for a spell. Sometimes, after a night's sleep, the answers just wake up with you, see?"

She kissed his chest. "I think so, darling. But if you don't want to talk shop and you don't want to talk dirty, what's left?"

He chuckled. "Let's talk about you. Are you still mad at the he-male side of the human race?" he asked.

"Not present company, you big hairy thing. But I still say this world would be run more sanely if you brutes would let us women in on running it!"

He smiled and said, "The boys as sailed with the Spanish Armada or the heathens getting killed right now by sweet old Queen Victoria might dispute the notion that the she-male gun hand's all that gentle. But let's say I handed you a magic wand and told you to go ahead and change the world. What would you change first, the internal plumbing of your own sweet sex?"

She toyed with his limp shaft as she giggled and said, "I'm not so sure I don't like the way we're both built, at the moment. But I wouldn't know where to start, putting order into the mess you men have made of things up to now. My God, we don't even have a sensible calendar or a standard time!"

He shook his head. "They wouldn't let you, even if you women got the vote. Calendar printers has wives, too, you know. How many hats would they ever get to buy if you put all their husbands out of business? Any fool can make up a calendar more sensible than the ones they get to print new every year. I made one up myself, years ago, when I still thought common sense was what the general public wanted. Mine starts in spring, sensible, instead of the middle of winter. It has thirteen months of four seven-day weeks, each starting on a Monday, so you get to have the same day of the week for every birthday no matter how old you get."

She laughed. "Thirteen four-week months leaves you one day left over, dear."

He said, "Three years out of four it does. I calls it New Year's Day. Nobody never works on New Year's Day, anyway, and if you start with the first day of spring my calendar is the only one you'd ever need to buy. Anyone can remember a leap year, and the other three hundred and sixty-four days never has to be changed at all. That's why it'll never catch on. Think of all the printers it would put on the dole."

She laughed. "All right, but what about women's suffrage or standard time?"

"She-males may get to vote someday, though I doubt we'll ever live to see it," he said. "They been talking about standard time for years. But like calendar reform, there's too many vested interests against it."

"Why, dear? Surely nobody has to buy a new watch every year no matter what time it is. So who'd be put out of work?"

"Gents who print *timetables,* for one. Besides, the world is round and so it just *can't* be the same time everywhere.

140

For when it's high noon in London it has to be midnight in the Sandwich Islands. It's a pure fact of nature."

She said, "Silly. Nobody's ever said the whole world would have to keep the same exact time. But wouldn't it be a lot simpler if, say, these United States were divided up into three or four time zones, with all clocks set the same until one moved east or west a full hour?"

"Folks are used to having high noon when the sun where they lives is overhead direct," he replied. "I've heard railroaders fussing about the way they has to keep setting their watches back and forth as they travel east or west, and it's even caused some accidents, with one gent reading the timetable one way and another different. But, like I said, most folk are set in their ways."

She started to pump him harder as she coyly asked, "Do you think you could set this in *my* ways some more, darling? I don't give a damn what time it is, here or anywhere else. I think it's time for more loving!"

He said that sounded like a better notion than changing the world with a magic wand. So, in no time at all, he had his wand in her again and they were going at it hot and heavy when he suddenly gasped, "Oh, Jesus, I'm dumb!"

"You certainly are!" she complained as, still in her, he started feeling for his vest on the floor.

She asked what on earth he was looking for down there and he said, "Railroad timetable, of course."

"At a time like this, you idiot?" she gasped. "I want to *come* again, damn it, not go for a ride on a train!"

He held some of his weight on one elbow as he spread the timetable across her heaving naked breasts, still moving in her politely, but apparently not enough for her, judging from the way she was bumping and grinding under him. She groaned, "Stop that, you fool! Stop reading in bed and treat me right!"

He saw that the next train through Tucson wouldn't get

there for a spell and tossed the timetable aside to make up for his recent neglect as Erica sobbed, "Oh, yesss! That's much better! But you're still crazy as a loon, and. . . . Oh, faster, darling, faster! I'm commmmming!"

That made two of them. But as they collapsed in one another's arms she still seemed peeved enough to demand, "What on earth was that all about just now? I've never been so insulted in my life!"

He rolled off reluctantly and said, "If I hadn't been feeling so fond of you, I'd have lit out sooner. As it is, I got to get over to the depot on the double. For there's a south-bound long-haul freight heading south this very minute and I got other chores to tend before I catch it!"

He sat up and bent over to grope up his duds. Erica sat up too, looking tastier, to him at least, and said, "Damn it, darling! You told me there wouldn't be another train to Nogales today."

"There won't be," he said. "The train I has to catch swings east, towards El Paso, and El Paso time is about a *quarter of an hour later* than Tucson time!"

Chapter 10

Erica hadn't been able to read the timetable from her position on the bed. So she didn't know Longarm had told her a white lie about the train he meant to intercept. The timetable said it was a somewhat poky way-freight rather than a high-balling long-hauler, but a man just had to fib to womenfolk now and again if he ever expected to get a lick of work done.

The SP ran that particular train every other day between the Pueblo De Los Angeles and El Paso, casual. So he had plenty of time to send some wires and even get some answers before it could crawl its way to Tucson, over three hundred miles east of its starting point as the crow flew, and even longer by winding rail.

Marshal Cunningham caught up with him when he took the time to be polite about the coroner's report on the demise of Bounty Breslin. As Longarm was leaving, after signing in triplicate, Cunningham tagged along to ask where they were headed with that Winchester Longarm was packing. Longarm said, "There's such a thing as common courtesy to a fellow lawman and there's such a thing as telegraphing one's punches. So I'd best just say I mean to catch the next train headed for El Paso, and—"

"Longarm, there *ain't* no train to El Paso this evening," Cunningham cut in.

"I know the every-other-day Pullman passed through last night, for I was aboard it," Longarm said. "But there's a way-freight poking along the track even as we speak, and I'd best get over to the yards."

The older lawman kept pace with Longarm saying, "Do that slow freight go all the way to Texas? I've never paid much attention to the comings and goings of trains I can't *ride*. But I was sure it just wandered into the Dragoon Mountains a few miles and come back."

"That's a sister train. They take turns on the stretches of single track across the desert. One I'm after gets to El Paso along about three or four in the morning, depending on how many sidings it stops at to pick up or drop off freight cars."

"Do tell? Well, I'll leave word at the depot for my old woman, then. You know how she-males get when a husband packing a badge don't come home the usual time."

"That's the main reason I've never married up. But I've wired ahead for backing when I get off and you'd have no jurisdiction the moment you crossed the township line, no offense."

Cunningham grinned like a sly old hound who'd just sniffed coyote. "A lawman in hot pursuit has the right to arrest anybody anywhere and we *are* in hot pursuit, ain't we?" he asked.

Longarm grinned and said, "Lukewarm, I hope. I may need all the backup I can get if this hunch I'm playing is right, but it's only fair to warn you the odds is almost even that I'm on a wild-goose chase."

"Don't shit your elders, boy. You wouldn't be packing that Winchester if you didn't cotton to the odds better than that, and you'd be bringing along your possibles if you was heading home from El Paso. So let me see if I follows your drift. You got a lead on something or somebody in El Paso, and you mean to bring whatever it is back here so's you can arrest the rest of the gang somewheres along the Santa Cruz, right?"

Longarm said that was close enough and they moved on to the SP freight yards. As luck would have it, Cunningham spotted one of his deputies along the way and told him to tell the old woman not to worry about him fooling about with *other* women if he got home a mite late. Longarm noticed he didn't tell the deputy why or where they were going, and scored the older lawman a point for smart thinking.

The sun was long down and a pale moon was rising above the jagged desert peaks to the east by the time the way-freight followed the long beam of its headlight into the yards and hissed to a weary stop. Longarm and Cunningham walked down the trackside to meet it as a yard bull with a red lantern cut them off to ask what in thunder they thought they were doing on railroad property.

Cunningham's badge was already pinned to his shirt, so Longarm didn't bother to flash his own as he said, "We're bumming a ride in the name of the law."

"Not unless you clear it with the brakeman first, you ain't," the yard bull said. "You'll find him back in the caboose. Only he can say who might or might not even write on this train with chalk!"

Longarm said, "I know. Tell me something, pard. Do you catch many a hobo hitching a ride without such permission?"

The yard bull brightened. "Oh, I see, you lawmen are interested in bank robbers riding the rails after," he said. "The Arizona Rangers asked about that already. But I may as well tell you, too. We got orders to be more careful than

145

usual in desert country. The old SP ain't as mean as some may say, but they don't call this line the Octopus because it's open-handed about free rides. On the other hand, it would be pure murder to throw a 'bo off in the middle of the desert. So even the empties is kept locked and sealed between Riverside, California, and El Paso, Texas. That leaves the rods and the blinds but we check hell outten 'em at every stop. So I can tell you true that nothing bigger than a cockroach gets on or off this train and, if I see a cockroach creeping toward it, I'm supposed to *stomp* it!"

Longarm thanked him and moved on down the cars with Cunningham, noting that, in fact, every door handle was wired securely, with a lead seal crunched over the wires.

Longarm led Cunningham up into the caboose at the far end. As they ducked inside, a burly railroader who had to be the boss brakeman, since he got to sit with his feet up on the cold pot-bellied stove while his assistants were out looking for hot boxes and bums, said, "You ain't allowed in here, gents."

"Sure we are," Longarm said. "This here's Marshal Cunningham of Tucson and I'm Deputy U. S. Marshal Custis Long. We need a ride east and, as you know, there ain't an earlier train headed that way tonight."

"That may well be, gents. But this here's a freight train, not a passenger train, and I ain't got authority to carry passengers."

Longarm sighed. "I go through this bullshit a lot," he said. "So let me tell you how it works. We could argue some, but then I'd just get the local law to freeze this train on its tracks long enough for me to wire your headquarters. Then in an hour or so you'd get a wire from them telling you to act more hospitable and giving you hell for running late."

The brakeman frowned thoughtfully as he digested Longarm's words of wisdom. Then he nodded grudgingly. "You ain't gonna find it a comfortsome trip in this crowded caboose, but I never invited you along in the first place. How far up the line are you headed?" he asked.

Cunningham said, "El Paso, to make an arrest by the cold gray dawn," before Longarm could kick him.

The damage had been done and the brakeman was starting to act neighborly, so Longarm nodded and said, "That's close enough. Where do you want us to set?"

The brakeman waved expansively at the built-in bunks and fold-down tables and such all around and said, "Anywhere you ain't in our way. Me and my boys takes turns napping on a long haul like this one. But there's always two-thirds of us up at one time. So just shift your asses as need be and we'll get along tolerable."

Longarm and Cunningham found seats. A little while later they were joined by the three junior brakemen. After they'd all been explained to each other, a crewman called Slim told the head brakeman, "Engine crew says they's watered up and looking forward to getting laid in El Paso."

The big boss got grandly to his feet to step out on the platform with his own lantern and wave clearance to the engineer up front. The engineer tooted twice and they started with a considerable jolt. The boss brakeman looked disgusted as he resumed his seat, saying, "I don't know where in hell they recruit them pretty boys. Seems every kid in the country wants to be an engine driver when he grows up. But you'd think the company could wait until they did!"

Longarm, who knew more about railroading than the general public, smiled and said, "Most kids don't know the conductor or brakeman is the real boss of the train."

The buttering-up worked. The brakeman said, "Slim, put some coffee on for these lawmen. We face a long, tedious trip with no passing scenery worth mention to admire." Then he climbed up into the cupola to admire as much as could be seen of the moonlit car tops ahead. He looked sort of comical with his head and shoulders out of sight and his big rump perched on its high seat at everyone else's eye level.

Slim said, "We don't really put the coffee on in desert country. We takes it on warm now and again as we stop. So you may find this a might tepid."

Longarm tasted from the tin cup Slim handed him and said, "At least it's real Arbuckle. How long's it been cooling in the pot?"

"Couple of hours. It wasn't all that hot when they handed it aboard to us at Eloy."

Cunningham asked Longarm, "Wasn't Eloy where that breed you shot got on last night, Longarm?"

Longarm wanted to kill him, but there were too many witnesses, so he just shrugged. One of the other brakemen seated across from him said, "Hot damn! You're the gent as made old Smitty and that colored boy so rich! Put her there, pard! I admire a generous man!"

Longarm shook, but looked disgusted as he said, "Might have known railroaders gossip as much as the rest of us. It's all up and down the line by now, eh?"

Slim said, "Sure. It went on the wire when they unloaded the stiff at Dragoon to be embalmed and boxed. The company said it was all right for the crew to claim the reward, as long as they didn't fib to the *management*."

Longarm just buried his face in the tin cup as the others asked dumb questions about the shootout on the passenger train the night before. He finally said, "I wasn't there, official. But as long as you boys know so much, can anyone tell me if the four passengers that was in the car put in for part of the money, too?"

Slim frowned. "There wasn't four, Longarm," he said. "There was only *three*. Only three as owned up to seeing Smitty shoot it out with the rascal, leastways."

Longarm didn't say anything. Cunningham nodded and

said, "That surely answers a question, don't it? If one of the innocent-acting passengers was really with the late Digger Dawson, we know, now, why the bank job in Eloy was called off at the last minute!"

"Another gang member could have got on earlier," Longarm said. "On the other hand, the shy gent left over could have had his own reasons for not coming forward for a split. I'll ask him if I see his face when we finish rounding them all up. I'm tolerable at recalling faces."

Now that the cat was out of the bag, Longarm made no attempt to shut old windy Cunningham up as he explained to the train crew that they were going to El Paso to arrest bank robbers. Longarm wondered how he knew so much, considering the little he'd been told. But, like most gents seeing light at the end of the tunnel, the small-town lawman was all wound up and anxious to show how smart he was. So Longarm didn't argue when Cunningham said, "I was wondering how them stole bonds could have wound up in central Mexico without passing through Yaqui country. They've been simply moving 'em south from their real home base in El Paso. How did we just figure that was where they was hiding betwixt jobs, Longarm?"

Longarm decided it wouldn't hurt to say, "Had they been spending enough time to matter in the Santa Cruz valley they'd have had their watches set to *local* instead of *El Paso* time. The watch on the one I dropped just south of Tucson was running fifteen or twenty minutes fast. I didn't think much of it at the time, it being a cheap watch. But the one gunned by a townee in Maricopa got *his* watch stopped *exact,* and unless it was set El Paso the fool gang had started out to rob a bank after the local closing time. That made two owlhoots with their watches running wrong the same way. Last night the pocketwatch of Digger Dawson cinched it, but I was too dumb to put it together until almost too late. Between cheap innards and the confusing way each

149

county seat sets its own local time, a man gets *used* to strangers not having the same exact time as himself. But, once I got reminded, and studied on it some, I could see gents moving *north and south* along the Santa Cruz had no call to be off so consistent. Maricopa and Eloy time are only a few minutes off Tucson's. If the gang was based over Yuma way between jobs, their watches would have been running too *early* by about a quarter of an hour. So that let Yuma out. But they had to be holed up *some* damned wheres between jobs, and El Paso's the place their slow watch dials all pointed at!"

Slim said, "It only works part way, Longarm. I know all too well how complexicated local time is, for I damn near died in a wreck one time when the fool yardman in Needles set his watch by local time and throwed the switches wrong. But both you feds and the Arizona Rangers considered train-riding bandits right after the first posse lost them the first time in the desert, with tracks within less distance than water. Every train crew has been questioned blue in the face about it. And to date the SP has no record of selling a dozen tickets in a bunch out in the middle of nowheres."

Another brakeman chimed in. "And keep it in mind they was last seen mounted up, Longarm. A lady has been knowed to pass an overgrowed kid as a half-fare aboard the old SP. But any conductor punching a ticket for a *horse* would be likely to remember!"

Everyone laughed. Then Cunningham said, "Said horses would have been recovered, had they been abandoned in the desert. Some at least would know enough to head back to town for water, and those who didn't would have left a sky trail of buzzards for the posse involved. So these boys is right. However them rascals get back to the big city betwixt jobs, they has to take their mounts with 'em."

The talkative Slim was enjoying the detective game, now

150

that they seemed willing to let him play. "They asked us if it was possible for a gent to mayhaps bury a horse he'd stole in the first place, somewhere in say a dry wash, and just grab the irons of a passing freight," he said. "We told them it was possible to do anything with a used-up horse, but impossible to grab holt a desert freight, for more than one reason. Even a slow way-freight like this one don't move slow betwixt stops. We makes up the time we loses picking up freight by going lickety-split across the nothing-much everywhere else. The second reason is, as you can see, we always have a man up in the cupola whilst we're running. So, even if some cuss could run across open desert fast enough to catch a train doing forty miles an hour, he'd be spotted soon as hell and, if you ever mean to grab a passing freight's irons, don't try it on old Rooster, there! Hey, Rooster, tell 'em what you done to that nigger hobo just outside of Needles that time."

The boss brakeman growled down, "You talk too much, Slim. It's official record that black boy went under the wheels of his own volition, and I told you before the matter's closed!"

Slim chuckled. "Old Rooster gets flusterpated when we flatter him. But, anyways, don't never try to steal a ride on a train he's braking."

Longarm rose to help himself to more coffee.

"How do you reckon they sneaks back and forth from the Santa Cruz to Texas, Longarm," Cunningham asked him. "It has to be a quick way, if they don't bother to reset their watches between leaving home and getting back. But it don't work by rail and unless their mounts are big-ass birds it's at least two weeks' ride over mighty rough country. So they'd naturally pass many a local town hall clock reminding them to set their own pocketwatches ahead, and . . . That was stupid, wasn't it? They'd naturally ride nowheres near any *towns*, riding sneaky. It wouldn't matter exactly what their own dials read, as long as they all read the same all the time."

"That's the way us railroaders do it," Slim said. "You can wind up off the tracks, keeping different times along the same line. So we keeps our own railroad time. Each section decides what time it is *some* damn place and then we all sets our watches to agree with each other."

Longarm had already known that, but Cunningham asked what time it was on this section of the Southern Pacific right now. When Slim took out his own nickel-plated railroad watch the old lawman said, "Thunderation, I'm already way ahint you. For your watch seems to already be in El Paso!"

Slim put his watch away, saying, "Ever' railroad watch this side of Yuma is. Trains leave the Los Angeles yards on Yuma time, then change to El Paso time crossing the Colorado. If we kept time the other direction our watches would always be a mite early instead of a mite late. Saves arguing when a train's *really* running late, see?"

Cunningham voted with old Erica, even though he hadn't heard her views on standard time, as he shook his gray head wearily and said, "I'm glad I don't have to travel much. It's complexicated as hell." Then he turned to Longarm and asked, "Reckon we should set our own dials to jibe with where we're headed, even though we won't get there for hours?"

"I already have," Longarm said. Then, as the train slowed down, he took out his watch and timetable to ask, or rather tell Slim, "This here stop would be Patano, right?"

Slim said it sure would as he rose to pick up a bearing-box wrench and step out on the platform. The head man, Rooster, climbed down from his perch with a clip board and growled, "You lawmen best stay put. We're just picking up one empty here, and should you get lost in the bumping

152

and grinding we ain't got time to wait."

"Can I take it said car might be sealed as well as empty?" asked Longarm.

Rooster said, "You could. Company orders. Come along, then, if you don't believe me."

Longarm stayed put as he smiled up at the burly brakeman. "No, thanks. I can see nobody could possibly sneak aboard this particular train without your enthusiastic approval."

Rooster muttered under his breath and went on out. The others did the same, leaving Longarm and Cunningham in the caboose as, for the next few minutes, it got the hell bumped out of it while they spliced the new car on just ahead of them. Cunningham winced at a particularly nasty jolt and asked, "Jesus, do we have to put up with this all the way to El Paso?"

"It was your idea to come along, old son," Longarm said. "I should have told you a way-freight is a freight that stops along the way a lot. Most of the cars they'll be picking up tonight will be empties, bound back East after delivering pianos and such to small Arizona communities. Most of what you ship yourselves rides in open gondolas or cattle cars."

"I suspect I'll know more than I ever wanted to about railroading afore we gets to the end of the line. Who's meeting us there, the Rangers?" Cunningham asked.

"Rangers and at least one gent from the local county sheriff's department. It's considered polite."

"I know. After we pick up some backing, it gets more confusing. I see how you figured bandits keeping El Paso time had to be from El Paso. But El Paso is a big town, and Juarez, just a bridge span away, is even bigger. How the hell are we supposed to know where they are, once we get there? You didn't find a home address on any of the rascals, did you?"

"Not hardly. They was shy about even using their right names. But don't worry about Juarez. We don't have jurisdiction there, and I've got direct orders to stay out of Mexico."

"I don't want to visit Mexico either till they get a more sensible government down that way. But as the mists clear from these weary old eyes, it do seem logical that our El Paso-based gang has to be smuggling them stolen bonds into Mexico via the crossing at Juarez. Damn it, Longarm, you're holding something back on me, ain't you?"

Longarm nodded and said, "Sort of. I think it was old King Henry VIII who said two could keep a secret if one of them was dead."

"In other words, you *do* have an address to lead us to, but you mean to hold it close to your vest until the time comes?"

"That's close enough."

"All right. I can wait. But I sure can't figure out how nothing but some pocketwatches set wrong gave you the exact place to go to in a town as big as El Paso. Are we talking about some she-male like Belle Starr who hides such cusses out regular in El Paso? You could have connected one of the dead ones to a knowed lover-gal. Yeah, that works."

Longarm chuckled and said, "If only life was so easy. If any such records was to be found, the case would have been cracked long before I got here. But don't strain your brain, pard. For, as the old song says, 'Farther along we'll know all about it. Farther along we'll understand why.'"

"Jesus, it ain't enough I got to ride all the way to El Paso jolt-assed, I got to listen to Sunday-School hymns, too!"

The brakemen started piling back aboard. As they settled down, Slim looked about and asked, "Have you gents seen

154

Rooster? We're all hooked up and ready to roll. He must be taking a piss or something."

Longarm rose, picked up a lantern, and stepped out on the platform to swing it for the engine crew. As the engine tooted twice and the train started up with a jolt Slim gasped, "Have you gone loco, Longarm! *You* can't start this train!"

"I already have," Longarm said. "One of you better get topside. *I* wouldn't know what to do if I saw something out ahead."

"I got to hit the infernal *brakes!*" Slim said. But Longarm drew his .44 and said flatly, "Don't, Slim. That's an order, in the name of the law!"

Slim froze as good as anyone else might have, but almost whimpered, "You *must* have gone loco! I know you boys are in a hurry, but if the line don't fire us all for leaving Rooster behind, he'll kill us when he catches up! What you just done would be the same as tossing the captain of a ship over the side, only more serious! I've been railroading a good ten years and I ain't never heard of a train going *nowheres* without its *brakeman* aboard!"

Longarm said, "You're a brakeman. So I'm putting you in charge, Slim."

Slim gasped, "Bullshit! Nobody but Mr. C. S. Huntington in the flesh could treat his Southern Pacific so disgusting and get away with it. You may be a federal lawman, but right now you're bending the shit outten federal railroading law, Longarm!"

Cunningham had said he'd back Longarm, so his own hand was resting on his own gun grips. But he had to say, "I sure hope you know what you're doing, son."

"If I didn't, I would be doing it," Longarm said. "There wasn't time back there to look for Rooster, and Slim here's a qualified brakeman. So what the hell. Get up in the cupola, Slim. It's against regulations for a train to run *blind,* too."

Slim did as he was told, muttering he could likely get a job almost as good on the new Santa Fe, anyways.

Longarm sat down, but held his gun in his lap. The others just stared at him the way folk stare at a madman they mean to humor until someone can figure out what to do.

So the next twisty twenty-odd miles went by sort of tense as the way-freight wound through the rugged hills between Patano and Benson. Then Slim dropped down and said, "I got to signal the next stop. We got to drop off two cars on the next siding."

"I don't want you to," Longarm said. "Get back up there. I'll wave a highball out the side to the engine crew."

"You crazy son of a bitch! We got to stop at Benson! It says so, right here on the order board!"

Longarm just picked up the lantern again and when Slim looked thoughtfully at a nearby tool rack, old Cunningham drew his own gun. "You heard the man, sonny," he said. Then, as Slim got back up in the cupola with a fatalistic shrug, the old lawman sighed. "I sure hope he knows what he's up to!" he muttered.

Longarm did, too, as he signaled the engine to keep going while the light of the little desert town came to meet them up the track. The engineer slowed down but didn't stop as he signaled with his whistle to clear the switches ahead. As they rolled slowly through Benson yards, some other gents with lanterns stared up at Longarm, slack-jawed, and then they were crossing the trestle over the San Pedro and picking up speed as they went through the twin town of Pomerene and hit open country again.

They crossed the Dragoon range, and this time Slim didn't argue when he was ordered not to stop at either the town of Dragoon or tiny Cochise. But one of the other brakeman warned, in the tone one uses on crazy men or unreasonable women, "I know you boys are in one hell of

156

a hurry to make El Paso. But if we get too ahead of schedule this trip could end with one hell of a bump!"

Longarm nodded. "I'll signal the engine to slow down. What's it look like up there, Slim?" he asked.

"Cactus flats, of course. Wait a minute. I see lights ahead, and . . . what the hell, we *can't* be coming to Wilcox yet!"

Longarm leaned out to signal a coming stop. Then he ducked back in and said, "You boys better get to work on the brakes. I just saw the same fires, and they ain't that far."

The other brakemen piled out of the caboose, only too happy to get away from their lunatic passenger, as Slim called down, "What in hell is going on, Longarm? We're out in the middle of nowheres and some assholes has lit a ring of bonfires around the tracks!"

Longarm said, "They ain't assholes, Slim. They's Arizona Rangers and some gents from Cochise County. I wired ahead for 'em to meet me here." Then he stood up and added, "Hand me down that order board. I need it."

As Slim obeyed, old Cunningham rose, drawing his own gun, to ask, "Can I open my present now, Mama?"

Longarm holstered his pistol and picked up his Winchester from its corner with his free hand as he said, "Sure, come along, little darling."

So, as the train ground to an unscheduled halt in the middle of a salt flat, the two lawmen jumped down to be greeted by a mounted Ranger captain who bawled out, "All right, Uncle Sam, here we are and here you are, so what in hell happens next?"

Longarm raised his voice to be heard on both sides of the halted way-freight as he called out, "All you boys on my side cover all them so-called empty freight cars while I see which seal we ought to bust first."

He started up the line, reading off the clipboard as old

Cunningham and the mounted Ranger tagged along. Long-arm muttered, "This one's from Yuma. This one has been standing empty at Maricopa two days, under a hot sun. But this little piggy was picked up in Eloy late this very afternoon and, yep, here's one that don't work, neither."

Then he turned back to the dusty barn-red car the way-freight had gathered from the Eloy yards about the time he'd been having more fun with Erica. After signaling the others to stand clear of the only way out, he rapped the side of the car with the muzzle of his Winchester and said, "There's two ways we can work this, gents. You can come out peaceable with your hands full of stars, or we can just punch bulletholes through that thin wood till none of you are in any condition to make a choice. It don't matter to us one way or t'other, but I feel sorry for your horses, at least."

The owlhoots inside, after some brief whispered discussion, must have thought they had a better notion. For the door slid suddenly open, breaking the flimsy wire seal, and eight mounted men jumped their horses out like unsprung cuckoo-clock birds, one right after the other, shooting wild in every direction, and yelling fit to bust.

It didn't work, of course. Longarm and the other lawmen he'd set up so nicely had the advantage and took it as the confused bank robbers piled out the one door, some spilling right away as their mounts were surprised to be galloping a good four feet or more off the ground.

One managed to land at full gallop and make it almost to the fire line before a deputy from Cochise County earned the right to bore his grandchildren likely well into the next century with the tale of how he'd nailed his target directly between the eyeballs, shooting from the hip.

All but two had similar luck, and one of the whimpering survivors clawing sky surrounded by grinning lawmen was hit bad in the hip. Longarm dropped the clipboard and strode over to the one who was groaning less, saying, "I don't really have to tell you you're under arrest. So now you'd best tell me who's missing here. We was hoping to find a dozen of you."

The captured bank robber winced as someone unhooked his gun rig, brutal, and sighed, "You got us all, Longarm. Old Pete's luck run out at Maricopa, and you know damn well you gunned old Digger last night."

"Well, ten might look like a dozen to a rattled witness used to counting eggs more'n bank robbers. But ain't we forgetting some? Never mind about Rooster. He don't figure to get far on his own, with every railroader knowing his face and having him down as a renegade now."

The owlhoot shrugged and said, "All right. Anyone can see you has it all figured out, and the railroader working with us wasn't kin, anyways. Can I put my hands down now? I hurt my shoulder, dismounting head-first just now."

"After you clear us some more details, sonny," Longarm said. "If we take your word this was the whole active part of the gang and that Rooster was aiding and abetting you by leaving empty cars along the sidings sort of strategic for you, we still have the matter of them stolen government bonds winding up in Mexico."

The owlhoot looked sincerely confused in the firelight. "Bonds? What bonds?" he asked. "I don't know what you're talking about. No shit, this shoulder's really killing me."

Longarm nodded to the Ranger behind the prisoner and told him to lower his hands behind him for cuffs. As the prisoner was led to the buckboards the Rangers had brought, to ride back to their nearby post along with the dead and dying, Longarm turned to old Cunningham and said, "That about wraps things up here. We just have to ride on to Wilcox and there'll be time for a few drinks before we catch the late-night train back to Tucson, unless you know some gals in Wilcox. I don't have to explain tedious how these wayward youths got to ride both ways, too, with a brakeman in cahoots with 'em?"

"Let's see if I got it straight," Cunningham said. "They was holed up just outside the Santa Cruz valley, but living on *railroad* time all the time?"

"You're catching on. Time you grow up you'll make a fair lawman."

As they started back for the caboose, Cunningham said, "Hold on. This case is far from wrapped entire, Longarm! You didn't believe that son of a bitch when he denied knowing anything at all about more than half the loot from the Maricopa job, did you?"

"Sure. Why not?" Longarm said. "He was badly shook up, and they figure to throw the book at him no matter what tale he tells now. So why should he want to fib to the arresting officers? He's an old pro. He knows his only chance of a reduced sentence would be full cooperation. So, it's my considered opinion he has no more to tell us."

"Then who in thunder *did* ride off with them government bonds?"

"Beats the shit out of me," said Longarm. "I'm still working on that."

Chapter 11

By the time they got back to Tucson, Rooster had been picked up in Tombstone and, like his namesake, was crowing loud and clear. The wire from Marshal Earp in Tombstone just verified some loose ends Longarm had already figured. After unloading their mounts from a so-called sealed and empty box car left in the nearby yards by old Rooster, the gang had just ridden out in a cloud of dust, leaving mighty few tracks crossing gritty railyards, and simply snuck *back aboard* to lie doggo until they could be picked up and delivered somewhere else, far, by their confederate. The reasons they'd been hitting banks late in the afternoon, of course, was that even three or four hours in a box car under an Arizona sun could get mighty stuffy. But the work had paid well, up until recently. The late Digger Dawson, after scouting the bank at Eloy, had meant to pass the coded information on to Rooster, up the line. Once Rooster had heard other railroaders talking about the shootout, and knew the simple coded message was in the hands of the law, he'd warned the boys, of course. But since they'd already been hauled to Eloy by rail on schedule, they'd just had to sit tight there till Rooster could come back for them, as Longarm had hoped they might.

Longarm didn't want to be seen sneaking into a lady's house at daybreak, so he waited until office hours before looking up Erica, for two reasons. The first reason was that she wanted him to lay her some more and she found it new and novel to be laid atop her office desk. The second reason was that he had to confront young Willy May Bronson with some photographs, not all of them pretty, and thought it best Erica be there as both her lawyer and another woman. So Erica got dressed again and, as they rode out to the Double B in her buckboard, she asked if she could see the pictures first.

Longarm took the packet out. "Most of these was took last night," he told her. "Some earlier. See anyone you know?"

She handed him the reins as she leafed through the pictures, grimaced, and said, "They're all total strangers to me, thank God. For I sure wouldn't want to meet some of them in the dark!"

She handed them back and he put them away. Then she counted in her head. "Wait a minute, Custis," she said. "You say there were ten men in that gang, not counting the crooked railroader who was covering for them. But you seem to have a dozen pictures there."

He nodded. "Ten's accounted for, including the one killed robbing banks and the breed I brushed with on the train. I showed these other two gents to the surviving gang members. They both swore they'd never seen either before. I didn't think a rat like Bounty Breslin would go in for stand-up bank robbing. The girl says one of the men who must have killed her brother was stocky and sneaky-looking. But she said they was both smooth-shaven, and the rascal I gunned not far from here on this very trail wore a moustache.

162

But she may be able to narrow it down some if she can identify Breslin."

Erica asked, "Wasn't the man trailing you out here keeping El Paso time with his watch, too, darling?"

"He was keeping railroad time, same as the gang, but that don't mean he was anything but a man interested in train connections," Longarm answered. "Some damned body had to have carried them stolen bonds all over Robin Hood's barn, leaving a false trail as more of 'em made it to central Mexico to get cashed more serious."

"I'm beginning to see what they must have been up to. They certainly were cold-blooded, duping poor Bucky and then trying to frame him after killing him! They were hoping all the time you'd ride on down to Nogales, right?" she asked.

"Yep. They dragged a red herring down here, south of town and the rail connections to more sensible places. By cashing another bond in Nogales and then likely abandoning the ponies they got from Bucky to return by train within hours, they aimed to help me lose myself in a mighty rough neighborhood. I don't know if the one I shot was just covering the kid's ranch to see what I done and, seeing a chance to gun me, tried to, or if I just shot him sort of by accident. Never chase an armed gent through prickly pear waving a gun of your own unless you know him mighty well."

Erica steered the conversation back to sex as they drove on, so after they'd talked dirty a spell they were at the Double B.

Young Willy May insisted they come inside and try the corn cakes some of the Papago gals had been teaching her to make before she would even look at the pictures. Longarm was pleased with Erica for being such a good sport. He knew lots of Indians found wood ash flavorful but some white gals could act snooty about it. Once they'd both agreed they loved her cooking, he put Willy May to work on the

163

photographs. She spread them across her checkered table-cloth and asked, "How come some of them are staring at the camera so funny?"

"They was lying down to have their pictures took," he said. "Have you ever laid eyes on any of these rascals, standing up or otherwise?"

She pointed at the picture of the dead Bounty Breslin. "This looks like one of the men my brother had dealings with. He was the sneaky-looking one I mistrusted from the first!"

"You had good reason to, Miss Willy May. How about this other one, with the moustache? You said your brother rode into town with two of 'em, remember?"

"I remember telling you that, but I don't remember this man at all. The one with this mean-looking gent was younger and cleaner-cut. He was smooth-shaved, and I mind thinking how nice it might be should he come calling some other time."

Longarm gathered the pictures together as he nodded and said, "Well, you did say it might have been two or three. Old Moustache likely rode picket while his pals came in to razzle-dazzle your poor brother. The late Bounty Breslin had to look me up in town, meaning he was elsewhere when I got here, meaning he was likely the one who ran the stolen bonds over to El Paso or beyond to sell in Mexico. By now they've cashed 'em all. But of course Uncle Sam won't hear of many before they've matured to full interest. I'd say the crooks sold 'em in Mexico for a third face value. Not a bad profit, when you consider how little the rascals paid for them in the first place."

"Custis found out the bonds were carried off in the green box they planted here to make your brother look bad," Erica told the girl. "But we know now that Bucky was innocent as the day is long. Isn't that right, dear?"

"Well, he was too innocent for me to bother with in my

official report," Longarm said. "What do you two gals mean to do with this spread, now that nobody figures to dig it up no more?"

"We have it up for sale," Erica said, "but there's no hurry. I'm not sending Willy May back to California without a handsome dowry, and the price of real estate keeps rising every day in Arizona, now that the depression of the Seventies is over."

"Don't hold out too long." He shrugged and added, "Them depressions has a way of coming back every few years. But, yeah, you ought to get her a good price with beef starting to boom and that silver panic settling down."

Willy May followed them back outside and waved goodbye to them wistfully as they headed back to town. Erica asked if he wanted to go back to her office or direct to her house, explaining, "That desk blotter was sort of interesting, but I'd really rather have two pillows under my poor behind, you brute!"

He chuckled. "Hold the thought. I got to run down to Maricopa on the next train, and unfortunately my timetable says there's an early freight bound north before noon."

Erica sighed. "How soon before noon, darling?" she asked. When he said eleven forty-five she said, "It can't be ten yet," and commenced to run her carriage horse cruel as hell for such hot weather. But Longarm didn't tell her not to. He could see she was sort of hot as well.

The train he caught north was running late, fortunately, but Longarm made it to Maricopa before the banks closed. He found old Tom Marino on duty near the door. The bank guard was sober, this early in the afternoon, but looked mighty worried as he said, "Thank God you came here first, son. There's a gent making war talk about you along Saloon Row. His name is O'Hanlon. Young, nice-looking gent when he's sober. Meaner than a spotted skunk when he's drunk, which seems to be most of the time."

Longarm nodded. "I know Laredo O'Hanlon. But what's he doing down here in Maricopa? Last I heard, he was working as a bodyguard for Banker Mansfield, back up the line in Tucson."

"Not no more," Marino said. "He got fired, likely for filling his own body with too much booze to guard *others* worth a hang. Anyhow, he seems to blame *you* for some fool reason, so consider yourself warned."

"I will, and I thank you. But that's not why I'm here. I wanted to talk to your boss, Banker Jenson."

"We heard about you and the Rangers rounding up the bank robbers last night. He's pleased as punch, but he ain't here. You just missed him. He had to go off somewheres on business."

Longarm stared past the old man at the oak and brass bank of teller cages and said, "You may be able to answer some of my questions, Tom. When you all got held up that time, do you recall a green stongbox vacating the premises about the same time?"

The old man looked sheepish and said, "To tell the truth, I was staring at the floor a lot, crouched under yon table. But, now that you mention it, I do recall what looked like an old Wells Fargo strongbox dragging past me across the floor."

Longarm sighed. "Ain't it awful how some kids fib? It's getting so's you can hardly trust nobody. I'd like an intro to the others here on duty that day, for unless you're mistook about that green box, there goes the soap again."

The bank guard led him to a sort of secret panel, save for being marked "PRIVATE" to keep bank robbers from missing it, and they went behind the tellers' bars. Like most banks, this one was less imposing backstage, and could have used a coat of paint as well as a good cleaning. The two male tellers came to join them and both, alas, recalled the bank robbers leaving with the green box as well as a gunny sack one had been stuffing with the more petty cash from their drawers. "They made the boss open the safe in his office," one said. "Helt a gun to Miss Tillie's head."

He was just about to ask who Miss Tillie might be when the door of the banker's inner sanctum opened and a familiar face peered out to ask what was going on. She recognized Longarm at the same time and said, "Oh, it's you!" in a flustered tone.

Old Tom introduced her, anyway, as Miss Tillie Simmons, the boss banker's "sexy-terry," as he put it. Longarm wasn't sure the old man wasn't sounding innocently ignorant on purpose. For the bank guard was a sort of sly old dog, and the last time Longarm had seen this particular gal she'd been in the company of Peggy Gordon at the Silver Sombrero Sporting Saloon. She was the younger, darker, prettier female who'd been with Banker Jenson.

She looked more wholesome this afternoon, wearing calico and a pencil in her pinned-up hair. So he decided to take her at face value as she invited him in, shut the door after them, and asked what his pleasure might be.

He explained he'd really come to discuss the still missing bonds with her boss or whatever. Tillie blushed becomingly and said, "I suppose you're wondering what I was doing in that awful place the other night."

He shrugged. "If you really work here, it's safe to assume you was just a guest *there,* right?"

She made a cute little grimace. "Danny and I had to entertain that awful old Mr. Mansfield from Tucson. I'd never have agreed to go along if I'd known that terrible woman would be there."

"I've been dragged into awkward social situations, too. Would Danny be your boss, Jenson, and is he just your boss, or somebody closer? I ain't trying to be nosy, ma'am. I just like all the cards on the table."

She looked away and said, "We're not exactly spoken for one another, if that's what you mean. But we do go out together now and again after hours. Is that a crime? We're both young and single, you know."

"I know the feeling. I thank you for clearing the air, ma'am. So now let's get down to the business I come to see old Danny about."

"He's not here," she said. "He had to drive out to a homestead to see about a second mortgage or, rather, he had to drive out to see if the place was still *there*. You've no idea how many people try to borrow on a place they've stripped, meaning to move as soon as they bilk the bank for yet more money."

"Homesteaders say mean things about you folk, too, but I reckon there's good and bad in every breed. How soon are you expecting him back? Your clock out front says you're fixing to close soon."

"Oh, we'll be working back here until well after five," she said. "Mayhaps even later. Even with the loan from Tucson we've a lot of bookkeeping to catch up on."

"But your front door will still be locked after three, won't it?"

She nodded and moved across the room to unbolt and open a solid oak door leading out to the back alley. "The front door's just for the general public, of course. If you come around the back and knock on this door, say around four-thirty or five, I'm sure Danny will be back by then. I'll tell him you're coming, so I'm sure he'll be waiting if you're a little late. If he's not here when you get here, *I'll* just have to entertain you until he arrives."

She shut the door and came back around the desks to lean against one, closer to him, as he studied on her exact meaning. For both her words and the smoke signals in her big hazel eyes could be taken more ways than one.

He said, "I'll try to get here early, Lord willing and the

creeks don't rise. While I'm still here, there's been some debate about what them bank robbers carried out of here that other afternoon, Miss Tillie. One of the few of 'em in condition to discuss their past misdeeds assured me they never carried off that green box filled with bearer bonds. But the boys outside said they did. So it's your turn."

She shot him a puzzled smile as she waved at the waist-high safe off to his side. "I was standing about where you are now, with a gun muzzle tucked behind my left ear. Danny knelt, right *there,* and opened the safe. I was too scared to recall every detail, but I distinctly remember one of them asking Danny what was in that old Wells Fargo box. He told them it was just filled with papers they wouldn't be interested in. They said they'd be the judge of that, and they took everything but some dust and a paper clip from the safe."

She repressed a shudder as she added, "One of them wanted to take *me* along as well. But, thank God, a nicer one told him not to be silly."

"He was more likely sensible than nice. They had enough trouble getting out of here with the loot, thanks to another gent I'd best talk with. I thank you for exposing a big fibber, and I'll be back around five, Miss Tillie."

As she let him out, she asked exactly what he wanted with her boss and sometime boy friend, Dan Jenson. He told her the fool regulations said he had to get a statement from everybody before he could write up his final report. She said she'd expect him around the back before sundown.

Longarm thanked old Tom out front, suggested they might have a drink on it later, and went across to the hardware store facing the bank.

The hardware man who'd smoked up one of the bank robbers had told his tale so many times by now that he was starting to pin extra medals on himself. But Longarm listened politely until the merchant got to the old bullshit about,

"I hated the thought of taking another human life, but it was him or me!" before he cut in to say, "I can see how ashamed you must feel, sir. But what I really want to know is, did you see anyone packing a big green box amid all the confusion of your single-handed shootout with the desperadoes?"

The hardware man scratched his head. "I seen one with a gunny sack. Not the one I shot, of course, and . . . By jimmies, two of them *did* ride out packing a foot locker or chest of some kind between 'em. Can't say what color, though. Everything was sort of dark outlines amidst all the alkali dust and gunsmoke."

Longarm said that was good enough and started to leave. Then he turned back and said, "I know this ain't my business, pard, and I hope you won't take it unkindly. But as one man who's been in a shootout to another, I'd skip that part about feeling so awful, after. I know you're *supposed* to. But *you* know you *don't*. It feels a hell of a lot better to *win* a gunfight than to *lose* one, and most gunslicks know this."

"Damn it, are you calling me a liar, you young squirt?"

"No, sir. It's a matter of official record you stood up to armed men with a gun and come out the other side alive. But, you see, so many old soldiers who never heard a shot fired in anger tell that same old tedious tale of it being them or him, that lots of meaner-hearted cusses tend to dismiss it as so much wind. Now that you got a rep as a gunfighter, you don't want some cynical young cuss thinking it might be safe to build his own rep on you. So, if you don't aim to take up gunfighting as a steady occupation, just grin like a shit-eating dog every time someone asks what it feels like to kill a man."

The hardware man said he'd study on Longarm's well-meant advice and they parted friendly. Longarm went to the

Maricopa Western Union to wire Billy Vail where he was now, in case he never got back to Denver alive.

By the time he'd polished off a bowl of chili and some apple pie as well it was after four. So he went to see which saloon old Tom Marino might be recovering from a hard day's work at the bank in. At the second saloon he tried he found Laredo O'Hanlon instead—or, from the sounds coming out of the fool, Laredo had found him.

The saloon hadn't been crowded in the first place, and it proceeded to get less so as Laredo whooped, "You'll not get outten it this time, Longarm! For you humiliated me in front of she-males and got me fired, and what have you got to say about that?"

Longarm bellied up to the bar and muttered, "For one thing, you was more sober the other night. So that might account for your better manners way back then. I'd like a beer, barkeep."

But the barkeep, for some reason, was headed for the back, carrying the cash till, running. Longarm smiled thinly at Laredo and said, "Guess this just ain't my day. Maybe if you'd stop yelling like a nanny goat in heat we could go some other place and get served, Laredo. I wanted to ask you some questions about Banker Mansfield, anyways."

"He fired me, cuss your eyes! He fired me because he said a bodyguard who turnt and run wasn't worth his pay, and it's all your fault! So fill your fist, you son of a bitch! A gunslick without a rep has nothing to live for. I gotta kill you to get back my self-respect!"

Longarm stared thoughtfully as well as coldly at the dead drunk bully. The trouble with the breed was that every once in a while they meant it, and Laredo *had* killed, at least once in the past. So Longarm said, "I want you to listen up, Laredo. There's nobody here but me to hear your brag, and I'm starting to find it tedious as hell. I can see by the way your boots is planted in the sawdust that you're giving serious consideration to some leather-slapping. Take my advice and don't try it."

But Laredo did. He was good, too, for a man so drunk. Laredo actually got his gun halfway out before Longarm could beat him to the draw, just, and poke a finger of hot .44-40 through his chest, deflating him a lot before he could hit the floor.

As Longarm stepped through the drifting blue haze to kick Laredo's gun the rest of the way clear, he caught a glimpse of his own somewhat ashen face in the mirror behind the bar and muttered, "All right, sometimes it *does* make you feel sort of sick. But don't do that no more. You ought to know by now how many piss-ants like Cock-eyed Jack McCall can really work up the nerve to draw on a man like Hickock, given enough redeye and time to brood!"

Naturally the noise attracted attention outside, and naturally the town law rushed in, gun handy. But by then Longarm had reloaded and pinned on his own silver shield. The Maricopa deputy stared down at the remains of Laredo and said, "Oh, that one. Figured we'd have to bury him sooner or later. You're the one they call Longarm, right?"

Longarm said, "I am. I'm here on more important matters. So why don't we get direct to a statement for me to sign for you? I fear there was no papers on this poor asshole, so I can't offer you anything but my sincere thanks for tidying up after me. But I'll pay for his box out of my own pocket. I've been lucky at...ah...cards of late, anyways."

The town law stepped over to the bar and got out his notebook as he yelled for the barkeep by name. As the barkeep poked a wary head out from between the curtains at the far end, the town law said, "Get us some beer, damn it. It's hotter than hell outside. How do you want this to go to the county, Longarm, self-defense or suicide?"

"Well, suicide might be stretching it some. I think it was me he meant to die. But he was so likkered up it was hard to tell just what he had on his mind."

The town law said, "Suicide is shorter to write and makes as much sense as drawing against a man with your rep, drunk or sober. Since you was the only witness, I'll put down the cause of death as self-inflicted whilst drunk. Did the poor cuss say why he was so filt with anguish, Longarm?"

"He did say something about getting fired and having slim hopes of finding another, Deputy."

"Hell, that's reason enough for a useless cuss to want to die. Sign here. I'll get some boys to carry him over to the undertaker's."

Longarm scanned the short report as he sipped at his long, cool drink. It was a mite casual, even for Arizona Territory, but he was running short on time, according to his home office, so he signed it. The town law came back in with a couple of gents who said they had nothing better to do. Longarm bought them drinks, too, and handed the town law two twenty-dollar double eagles for the undertaker. Whether the undertaker got it all or any part of it was no concern of Longarm's now that Maricopa had taken the body off his hands, official.

Chapter 12

Less than an hour later, Longarm was free of local discussion about Laredo's demise. But it took him longer than planned to find old Tom Marino, and when he finally caught up with the bank dick in a cantina on the wrong side of the tracks the old cuss was even drunker than Laredo had been, albeit a lot more friendly. The wine this cantina served was better than the last, so Longarm really drank his this time as he brought old Tom up-to-date. "Hired guns like Laredo usually don't have so much trouble finding work in these parts. Not according to the late Bounty Breslin," he told the bank guard.

Marino stared sort of glassy-eyed down at his own drink to reply, "Hell, Laredo was all talk. At least, everyone *thought* he was. He come to the bank looking for my job, after that other banker fired him. The boss told him not to be silly. Laredo must have gone *loco en la cabeza* to try for *you*, Longarm!"

"Yeah, better men have hesitated, with better reasons for fighting me. But let's talk about real gunslicks, Tom.

I've reason to suspicion there's one left over. Young, good-looking, dressed cow, and innocent-looking. He was with the late Bounty Breslin when the Bronson boy was murdered up in Tucson. Laredo almost fits, but I dunno. I can't see an old pro like Breslin wanting such a wild drunk riding with him. Ain't sure Laredo didn't have an alibi for the day of the killing, neither."

"How come? Nobody saw who killed the kid exactly, did they?"

"No, but Laredo was well-known around Tucson. Too well-known for the peace of such a small community. The dead boy's sister might or might not have known the bully of the town. But I can't see a pro like Breslin riding out to the Double B with him anyway. So let's clear our minds of Laredo's fair features and see who's left."

The old man shrugged. "Ain't seen many hardcased strangers or many strangers at all since the holdup, weeks ago. Maricopa's even smaller than Tucson and I know most of the folk here on sight, whether they want to talk to an old Mex or not."

Longarm saw he was getting moroseful drunk, too. So he called the not-bad-looking cantina gal over and confided, "I got to get him home to bed. You wouldn't know where he's staying since he got kicked out of the hotel, would you, señorita?"

He saw the hesitant look in her eye and snapped a silver dollar on the blue-washed table as he added with a wink, "Bet you a buck you don't know."

She smiled and said, "You lose, *caballero*. We let him use the lean-to out back. But you will have to carry him. From the smell, I fear he has already soiled himself again, eh?"

Longarm sighed. "When you're right, you're right. But I can drag him under the arms, safe, if you'll but lead the way."

The friendly cantina girl dropped the silver dollar down the front of her blouse with a wink and they soon had old Tom stretched out on gunny sacking under a brushwood shelter behind the 'dobe cantina. She said she got off duty at sundown. He said he'd study on it, but meanwhile he had to get the poor old cuss out of his soiled duds. So she left, saying something that sounded sassy in Spanish about sundown being the time when her church bells chimed.

After he'd bedded the old man down, Longarm headed back to the main street, consulting his watch. It was set on local time, as he assumed the local banker's would be, and it was well after five-thirty now.

But he didn't go around to the back of the bank. He walked innocently up to the front, glanced back and forth to see he had the walk to himself, and eased the front lock open with one of the keys he'd helped himself to while helping the old bank guard out of his pants.

There was nobody out front. There wasn't supposed to be at this hour. Longarm moved on the balls of his feet, let himself behind the teller's windows with another key he'd seen the old man use earlier, and eased up to the office door, placing an ear against the panels as he drew his .44-40 with his free hand.

Inside, he heard a man's voice asking, "Are you sure he said five, honey? It's almost twenty to six now, damn it."

His secretary, lover, or whatever, replied, "He'll be here. If there's one thing I can tell you about Longarm, he's a man who means just what he says." Then, damn her, she added, "I'll go out front and see if I can spot him anywhere on the street."

Longarm tensed as the door popped open and Tillie popped out. Then he pistol-whipped her across the nape of the neck to drop her harmless as well as clear before stepping through the door, snapping, "Drop it, Jenson!"

176

The young, smooth-shaven banker didn't. He seemed frozen as a figure in a wax museum as he crouched sideways to Longarm behind an overturned desk with a sawed-off shotgun trained across the improvised barricade at the other doorway leading to the alley. Longarm thought it a mighty dumb ambush, but there seemed no end to desperate stupidity today. For when Longarm repeated, "Drop it," Jenson came unstuck and actually tried to swing the twin muzzles of his own weapon through ninety degrees of arc at a man who had the drop on him!

So Longarm's first round put a little blue hole in his forehead and blew Jenson's scrambled brains out the back of his skull.

There was obviously no need for a second round. Longarm turned away with a grimace of disgust and knelt to pat down the gal on the floor just outside for concealed weapons. She tried to use one of womankind's oldest weapons as she fluttered up at him weakly, grabbed his groping hand, and clutched it to her breast, sobbing, "Oh, save me! He has a gun!"

Longarm said, "You got nice tits. I'm sure you're a great lay. But you sure don't *lie* good. For the record, it's against federal law to take out even a *first* mortgage on a *homestead,* Miss Tillie. Telling me that rascal in there was out of town looking into a *second* mortgage was just silly."

She gasped, "I didn't mean a federal homestead claim, Custis. I just used homestead as a figure of speech, see?"

Longarm said, "I considered the scant possibility a gal who worked in a bank might be confused about her real-estate terms. That's how come I snuck in so polite just now. But we know how things just turned out when I come through the front door instead of the back like you told me to. That shot will attract us some company any minute, so we ain't got much time to talk. I want you to listen tight, girl. I may be able to get you off with a charge of simple criminal conspiracy instead of murder in the first degree. But not if I don't *like* you!"

She rubbed his hand harder against the softer parts of her chest as she sobbed, "Anything! Anything you say!"

He nodded and told her, "This is how I think it works. The bank robbery was just one of them things as happens to banks. You and your Danny Boy was as surprised as any other bankers that gang hit just at closing time. They made Jenson open the safe the way you said, and you were even telling the truth about them asking what was in the strongbox and him telling them it was just filled with paper of no use to them. After that it gets sneakier. They dumped the bonds out, not bothering to read the small print in their hurry. Then they filled it with the heavy silver coinage most small-town banks have to have on hand for folk who still recall Confederate bank notes with dismay."

"It was Danny's idea, not mine!" she whimpered.

Longarm said, "I ain't finished. I know what your Danny Boy's bright notion was, once the bank robbers tore out with the hard cash, leaving the two of you alone for the moment with fifty thousand in bearer bonds scattered all about. Hardly anyone ever thinks to search the desk drawers of a man who's just been robbed, and who was to say what them desperadoes might or might not have took with 'em? But now that the two of you had all that government paper to dispose of, you needed help. As a licensed killer who hunted crooks for banks a lot, old Bounty Breslin was the logical crook for Jenson to turn to."

"I didn't want to have anything to do with that awful man, I swear!"

"Save your swearing for the judge. It don't matter whether you *liked* your confederate or not. What matters is that Breslin and your Danny Boy aimed to leave a false trail before the bounty hunter went further afield to cash in them bonds at a discreet distance. So they picked up a duplicate Wells Fargo box—they're not hard to find—and tried to frame poor young Bucky Bronson. They damn near succeeded. The boy had a shady rep and wasn't well-known in Tucson. They duped him into cashing a modest bond they could spare, then left him dead on the Tucson trash dump for us to connect up with it. Let's see, now . . . Your Danny Boy, dressed cow, was the one who helped lure Bronson to his doom. Then he come back here to help you play victim as Breslin rode around leaving more trails while at least one other sidekick kept an eye on the Bronson spread. You want to tell me about the gunslick with the heavy moustache now, Miss Tillie?"

"I swear I don't know what his name was. He was just a friend of that nasty old Mr. Breslin. They hardly told me *anything*, Custis! Danny just said all I had to do was keep my pretty mouth shut and he'd smother me in emeralds."

Longarm chuckled and said, "I didn't take you for a genius, no offense. But I reckon that about wraps it up. For your Danny Boy wouldn't have been laying for me personal if he'd had any serious friends but you left at this late date. By the way, how much did he offer Laredo O'Hanlon in hopes of avoiding what just happened?"

"I don't know," she said. "They talked about *something* in private when Laredo came here looking for a job. But, wait! Laredo worked for that nasty old Mr. Mansfield! How do you know *he* wasn't up to something sneaky, Custis?"

"He is," Longarm said, "but I can't arrest him for it and his wife has her own way of punishing him. Banker Mansfield may be living a life too fast for his health, but he can afford it. He's really rich. You and your Danny Boy just *wanted* to be rich. So when you saw the chance to get rich at the expense of small investors who trusted you, you took it."

Someone seemed to be pounding on the door out front,

now. Longarm helped Tillie to her feet, saying, "We'd best let 'em in before there's busted glass as well as other messes to clean up in here. We don't want to confuse the court about minor details like Laredo. It ain't neat to change reports once they's signed official. I'll just work up a short and simple confession for you to sign before I wires the local federal authorities to come pick you up, Miss Tillie."

As he started to lead her out front, she asked, "Do you really have to send me to jail, honey? Can't you let me off with a suspended sentence or something?"

"It ain't for me to say, Miss Tillie. Mayhaps if you're as sweet and friendly to the judge they'll let you out by . . . oh, say 1920 or so."

She dug her heels in and cried, "Oh, no! I won't go to prison till I'm old and gray!"

"Look on the bright side, Miss Tillie. As of the moment, you're the only one in on the plot who figures to grow one day older."

"I won't sign any confession. I take back every word I just said, and it will be just your word against mine."

"That's your privilege, ma'am, if you don't want to cop a plea down from a hanging offense. You study on that while I lets the local law in. I can see right now you're too upset to talk sensible."

There was no sense reporting directly to the office when Longarm finally got back to Denver, it being within an hour and a half of closing time. So, after he'd stored his saddle and gear at his hired digs on the unfashionable side of Cherry Creek, Longarm paid a call on a more fashionable widow woman on Sherman Avenue to see if she still liked him. She surely must have, judging from the fancy supper she cooked for him, after, and how early she wanted to go to bed for keeps that evening. So, though he meant well, Longarm was a mite late getting to the office in the morning.

But, what the hell, he'd sent a full report by night letter before leaving Tucson.

As he went in, old Henry looked up from behind his typewriter and said, "Congratulations. The Treasury Department just sent you a citation about those bonds. Thanks to you pointing out that Breslin gent, they were able to trace his movements from El Paso to a Mexican bank that doesn't want another war with these United States, after all. So most of the bonds have been recovered, and you get a parchment scroll to keep and cherish."

Longarm snorted and said, "The cheap bastards might have sent me some tobacco, at least. I hardly ever smoke parchment. Big boss Billy in?"

"Surely you jest. It's almost ten, you slugabed."

Longarm chuckled and replied, "Oh, I wasn't just *laying* there, Henry." Then he went in to see how much hell Billy felt like giving him.

Marshal Vail didn't waste a thoughtful frown at the banjo clock on his oak-paneled wall *this* late in a working day. He growled, "Sit down and tell me how come. I know you pay no attention to clocks. But you might glance at the goddamned *calendar* now and again!"

Longarm took his usual seat and lit a cheroot as usual before asking innocently, "What's wrong, boss? You told me to take my time on that case."

"I did, and then I wired you soon after that the mess your fellow deputy was in had blowed over. I've read your wired-in report, and so I reckon you expect me to tell you that for once you done a fine job. But, damn it, old son, you turned that Simmons gal over to the Arizona Federal Office on the second of this month, and here it is almost the thirteenth! Where in the hell have you *been* all this time?"

Longarm settled back and took a drag on his cheroot before he smiled and said, "I had to pick up my stuff in Tucson and tidy up some other leftover details before I could leave the scene of the crime, boss. Funny you should mention calendars. One of my . . . suspects was mighty interested in calendar reform. But we got it all worked out by the time I managed to get out of Tucson alive."

Watch for

LONGARM AND THE COWBOY'S REVENGE

seventy-ninth novel in the bold
LONGARM series from Jove

coming in July!